'I read *Arrival* in on[e] [... the] narrator's need to flee her past, escape the confines of m[oth]anhood, and the stains of shame and guilt that keep repeating on her. The novel deals in life's hard knocks, in trauma and deracination, but in language that is sensual, languid, feline, snaking with double meaning and sly humour. Like a Sigrid Nunez novel, *Arrival* seems to be about everything, its canvas expanding and contracting, allowing the story's particulars to echo far and wide.'

MARINA BENJAMIN, author of *The Middlepause*

'A powerful tale about love, domestic violence, motherhood, escape, and arrival on many levels, written with sensuality and poetic force.'

NAJA MARIE-AIDT, author of
Baboon, Rock, Paper, Scissors and *Carl's Book*

'From the opening of *Arrival*, Nataliya Deleva demonstrates a remarkable talent for conjuring place and moment. It sits the reader beside her unnamed narrator. Whether in the Bulgarian valleys of her childhood or inhabiting the trauma-induced void that's replaced any semblance of home, we are beside her.'

HARRIET MERCER, author of *Gargoyles*

'*Arrival* is a book made up of fragments – fragments of love, motherhood, abuse and marriage – which form an intriguing and moving kaleidoscope narrative. A jagged, beautifully written novel which explores the shattering impact of abuse and how the past shapes the present.'

SAM MILLS, author of *The Fragments of My Father*

'This novel is a stunning achievement. It is a beautiful and moving story about trauma, memory, recovery, displacement and what it means to find a sense of home. An important story told with lucid, heartrendingly precise prose. I will come back to this novel again and again.'

LUCIA OSBORNE-CROWLEY,
author of *My Body Keeps Your Secrets*

'In her powerful second novel Nataliya Deleva explores the legacy of a childhood scarred by domestic abuse: how the confusion of love with pain creeps into every fragmented shard of adult life, contaminating relationships and complicating motherhood. Through the mythical *Samodivi* she conjures an enduring archetype of the wild rebel female who has escaped, who rejects the ways men control women. There is beauty and tenderness in the creation of her unnamed narrator's new life, in the poetry of survival and renewal, and in the breaking of patterns for her daughter – freedom from shattering cruelty.'

VENETIA WELBY, author of *Dreamtime*

THE

INDIGO

PRESS

ARRIVAL

ARRIVAL

NATALIYA DELEVA

THE
INDIGO
PRESS

THE INDIGO PRESS
50 Albemarle Street
London W1S 4BD
www.theindigopress.com

The Indigo Press Publishing Limited Reg. No. 10995574
Registered Office: Wellesley House, Duke of Wellington Avenue
Royal Arsenal, London SE18 6SS

This edition first published in Great Britain in 2022 by The Indigo Press

Nataliya Deleva asserts the moral right to be identified as the author of this
work in accordance with the Copyright, Designs and Patents Act 1988.

First published in Great Britain in 2022 by The Indigo Press

A CIP catalogue record for this book is available from the British Library

This is a work of fiction. Names, characters, places and incidents are
products of the author's imagination or are used fictionally and are
not to be construed as real. Any resemblance to actual events, locales,
organisations, or persons, living or dead, is entirely coincidental.

ISBN: 978-1-911648-37-6
eBook ISBN: 978-1-911648-38-3

Design by Luke Bird
Typeset in Goudy Old Style by Tetragon, London
Printed and bound in Great Britain by TJ International, Padstow

In memory of my grandmother

Motherhood is the place in our culture where we lodge – or rather bury – the reality of our own conflicts.

—JACQUELINE ROSE
Mothers: An Essay on Love and Cruelty

It's a fog-thick autumn morning. I am in a forest, playing a ball game with my granddad. I'm three or four years old. My mum has gone somewhere and I don't know where she is. I feel abandoned and scared and don't want to play the game. My shoes are wet from the dew and I can barely see anyway, so I cannot catch the ball when my granddad passes it to me, which starts to irritate him.

Then, suddenly, everything evaporates and I find myself all alone.

I don't remember anything else. It's just this heavy feeling of nothingness that envelops me and I feel almost strangled by my own anxiety.

This dream stayed with me for years. One day I came across a photo album and there, on one of the pages, was a picture of me in the forest, playing a ball game with my granddad. I froze. It was as though someone had entered my dream and captured a snapshot. A photo of a nightmare that had followed me everywhere.

§

I read in a book that children don't keep their early childhood memories unless they are constantly reinforced by family photos or stories. As if, during those first years, people don't exist. To me, memories are much more than a simple recollection of events. The fear erupted from the surface of my frangible consciousness long before I was able to construct reality with words or clear memories. It started at the edge of my body, crawled inside me, and stayed there for the rest of my life.

§

The following pages offer pieces of a story that can only exist in its fragmentation, in the randomness of events that, stitched together, create a delicate, almost translucent fabric, one that has wrapped my whole existence. Perhaps there was a narrative once, a continuing string of events. But now there are little particles of it, of me, spread around like atoms, as if someone has thrown a stone at a glass wall and broken it into pieces. Maybe I am the one with the stone, throwing it from my here and now. All I can do is collate the scattered pieces one by one, being careful not to cut myself.

STOP ONE
Estuary Wharf

No one must know about it. My mum had told me this so many times, the words had tattooed themselves on my fragile consciousness, and I carried them into my adult life. I grew into the woman I am today imbued with the facets of memories and overheard conversations that still linger and haunt. Unable to wash away the shame of what happened, I drag my parents' choices behind me like a sprained leg, convinced it was all my fault.

The only person I talked about it with, secretly, was my grandma. I spent most of my school holidays in the small village where my grandparents lived, climbing trees, picking raspberries and chasing fireflies when the darkness settled over our tired bodies. Surrounded by tall hills on all sides, the houses, viewed from above, must have looked like coffee grain sludge at the bottom of a giant cup. The days were long, and currents of dry scorching heat would leave marks on the twilight and into the evenings, when we'd all sit together in the porchway, slurping lentil soup with fresh garlic and home-made bread.

Taking a break under the vine trees in front of Granny's house in those late summer evenings, the grapes so full and brimming with sweetness it seemed to me they were about to burst, we would tell each other stories. Propped up on one elbow, I poured my nightmares into Grandma and she soaked them all up, taking in the heaviness of my words. Her face would change and the wrinkles would deepen in an instant, before she started whispering a fairy tale into my ears, her mellow voice like an emollient for my scratched mind. She would hug me, rub my back gently, and that was enough for my fear to dissolve. The secret, clutched between our bodies two generations apart yet pressed closely together, would remain untold to the world outside until the day I first met you.

I've always struggled to establish when things started. As a little girl, I used to think everything had a beginning, middle and end, though sometimes there were multiple endings possible, depending on the choices we made. But as I grew older, I became less certain of the beginnings, of the starting point from which events would unravel.

Sitting on the sofa in front of you, still tense during our first meetings, my mind slowly starts to sink into the softness of memories, deep into the stickiness of unsuspected feelings.

§

They were young and crazy in love, that's what they told me. He had dark hair and dazzling green eyes, which bewitched my mother the first time she looked at him. He loved playing his guitar and was the heart and soul of every gathering. She was fine-boned and dainty, with golden hair, a gentle look and a smile that would make the sun rise. They listened to the Beatles and believed in the freedom of choice.

That night was warm, like most nights in August in Sozopol. The gentle breeze brought in people's laughter and the smell of boiled corn on the cob, coming from a nearby street, the one with all the jewellery stalls, acrylic paintings and vintage clothes, and then it dissolved into the air. They were lying on the beach, snuggled in the dark, their bodies submerged in sand, in passion, in immensity like a cliché I cannot erase from the story of my own beginning.

When it became evident that she carried a baby in her womb, the sea backed away, waiting for her decision.

– Although I didn't want you back then, I learned to love you, my father once told me.

When did you start loving me, Dad? I never asked him this.

My mother's agony; twenty-one, third year at university, pushed to decide between the life of her unborn baby and the love of the man who wasn't ready to accept a child. Also, between graduating and building a career, and becoming a mother while studying at night and struggling to pay the bills. She had to find a way to keep both the baby and my father. I have no idea what she told him. A month later, they got married.

Each time I look at the pictures from the wedding, I gaze at their faces. Were they forcing themselves to smile for the photos, or did they feel happy?

I am also there in the photos, tucked deeply in my mother's womb, floating in my pre-existent guilt for everything which was about to follow.

§

Or maybe the story starts before they've even met.

The boy is eight or nine, perhaps. The football pitch is full of boys like him, socks up to their knees, knees wounded, wounds almost healed. The ones not playing are cheering from the sidelines. The players are the ones that matter, the future winners, the ones to admire if you're a girl, or if you care about those things. The boy fires the ball towards the goal, the opportunity is great, he thinks, it's now or never, he goes all in, the ball flies high, cutting through the air, above all the other players, and… score! That's it; he did it, three times *hurray*!

Just then, a little bruiser, annoyed with our boy, comes up from behind and pulls his shorts, yes, you heard it right, he pulls the shorts down. The world stops, it freezes before his eyes and then collapses. Children laughing, pointing at him, their faces looking so grotesque, but they can't see themselves. The only thing they see is the boy with his half-naked bottom.

From the depths of his shame the boy leaves the pitch, goes home, locks the door, and this memory stays inside him for the rest of his life.

The boy was my father. He told me that story once, when I said that I was sick of him getting drunk and humiliating me in front of my friends.

– You have no idea what humiliation is, he replied.

I know, Dad. I know.

§

It's not my child crying, and yet the scream perforates my brain. A raw, immediate cry that demands attention and comfort. Instinctively, I attempt to cover my ears, but abandon the idea and clutch the sides of the yellow chair I'm sitting on, legs crossed.

– The trauma unit is down the corridor. It gets a bit noisy sometimes, the receptionist says, noticing my brief move, and reaches for a sweet from the glass bowl on the counter, her nails the same colour as her ginger hair.

Just then you open the door. Your eyes meet mine for a brief moment, then swiftly crawl down and land on my daughter Ka, peeping from behind my back.

– Hello, pretty lady! Please come in, you smile, and your straight white teeth make me jealous.

I notice you. An Asian woman in your late forties or early fifties, well-kept, with long dark hair and a knee-length green dress that goes beautifully with your skin. The smell of freshly washed clothes engulfs me.

We step into your well-arranged but simple office. A small desk by the window, a white coffee table, a double sofa and an armchair in light blue fabric next to a bookshelf. Cushions in the same mustard yellow as the curtains. I remain standing by the wall, crumpling the side of the dark blue second-hand dress I'm wearing, which now feels glued to my sweaty back. Unfamiliar places always make me nervous.

– Please make yourselves comfortable, you say, inviting me to sit with a welcoming gesture, as though catching my thoughts.

I don't know how to make myself comfortable. I don't say this.

I sit on the edge of the sofa, picking the skin off my thumbs. You offer me coffee and I accept, since I notice the coffee machine; I can't stand instant. The aroma makes my senses tingle, reminding me that I should stay alert.

– There was no one to leave my daughter with so I had to bring her with me, I mutter, making an excuse.

You pull a jigsaw puzzle from the shelf and my girl's face lights up with impish glee. She grabs it, moves to one corner of the room and starts playing with it, while you leaf through my notes and take me through the frequency of the sessions and the process of booking them with reception.

Ka is only four but I fear that if she were to overhear us, the story would permeate her somehow and, without being able to fully understand my words, she would know. She would carry it with her like an unpleasant smell.

Then you prompt me to tell how I am feeling today, yesterday, the day before. Your words come gently, balming my fractured mind, but your eyes remain pinned on me. I know what you want. To peel off the layers of fear and anger and guilt to reach my remains, like fossils slowly revealing themselves, suggesting the life they've once contained. You wait. I smile but don't really. If I were still smoking, I would have needed to light a cigarette. You try to ease me into the conversation and say I should take my time.

I take my time. The silence starts to feel uncomfortable; I need to fill it with something, anything. The silence is like a too-big shoe. Where do I begin? How far back do I go?

– What are you afraid of?

The question brings me back to the room and I hear myself replying.

– Things I don't want to remember. Things I want to forget.

The eager look on your face makes me think this is not the answer you're after. The Dictaphone clicks and awaits my voice impatiently, like a lover. You wait for a story, so I give you one.

I am lying in my cot

in my fists I'm holding tight to the corner of the cotton blanket; its fluff sticks to my podgy fingers; I try to bring it to my face and put it in my mouth; I dribble and say 'ah goo'

the day slowly gives way to the night, the darkness occupies the room and my granddad turns on the table lamp; he is there, bent over the bed, smiling gently at me

I stretch my hands, trying to reach his gracious face; he can't resist the desire to hug the baby, his first granddaughter, and takes me in his arms; my face lights up, my two teeth, bottom ones, glint in the light and my granddad melts with happiness

he approaches the window; two doves are perched on the windowsill, rhythmically pecking the bread my grandmother had crumbled for them earlier; on the bookshelf next to it, there's a photo of my parents at their wedding, the one granddad used to show me over the years later, so that I don't forget their faces

someone rings the bell and my granddad opens the door, still holding me in his arms

– look who's back! mama

this is when I lock eyes with the woman by the door

mama; the word seems familiar but the face remains foreign to me; a brief, dim vision, an uncertain feeling that perhaps something has connected us in the past; mama is the word that my grandma and grandpa often say; they talk about her as if I was expected to know her well, to crave her presence when she's away and to long for her warmth when she's not around to hold me

the woman enters and, before even taking off her coat, she picks me up and cradles me tight but gently; she inhales deeply and stays like that with her eyes closed; the sweet smell of her skin next to mine makes me sleepy; she kisses my face, caresses my thin hair, touches my little nose with hers; I feel warm and snug, I don't want her to put me back in the cot, but she does

then she stays in the dark next to the window; the doves have pecked all the crumbs and have flown away; she is weeping; her silhouette throws a shadow over the curtains; my granddad curses his name, cries and hugs his daughter gently

you can't keep her away from her own choice: this is what I would have told him if I was able to speak

remaining silent in my bed, I breathe in the heavy air; my mother's sorrow merges with the helplessness of her father; a feeling of guilt has glued itself to my chest but I am too young to accept it as mine yet

sucking my finger, I dribble, but no one wipes it off my chin

– How are you feeling today?

– Detached. Distanced somehow.

– Tell me something. When did you decide to leave your country and come here?

– I don't know; there wasn't a specific moment. Some decisions take longer to emerge, but suddenly they unfurl and surprise us.

– Do you miss home?

– What is home?

– The place where you grew up.

– No, I don't.

– Why not?

– Because that home is fear. And guilt.

– And what is *here* then?

– Everything else.

§

Leaving my home country felt like escaping from prison. I was twenty-something, smitten with the idea of a life I'd never had. Those were the good years. It was like a breath of fresh air filling my lungs. I was taking it all at once: work, men, wine. For the first time, I was feeling free.

When I moved to London a decade ago, it took me ages to find a proper job. When I say *proper*, I mean a job where I used my brain, as opposed to other parts of my body. That's what my mother said at the airport the day I left.

Whatever you do, always use your brain.

In those first months, to pay my bills, I did all sorts of things. I distributed leaflets three days a week, cleaned an office on

23

Saturday mornings, made cappuccinos in a local coffee shop for a few hours on the busy days on when someone from the regular staff called in sick, and painted a fence (but didn't get paid for this, since the guy wasn't happy with my work). In the evenings I scrolled through the websites in search for a *proper* job, filled in forms, sent CVs and cover letters. After months of nervous searching and hundreds of applications, I was eventually offered an entry-level role at a small marketing agency with a quirky office next to a traditional English pub.

My manager's surname was Small and, whether this or something else in his life played a role in his insecurity, he would constantly assert his superiority over me. Whatever I said, he would ask me loudly to repeat it several times, pretending not to understand my accent. People would turn, some with obvious irritation that I couldn't speak the language fluently, others with a pitying smile.

One of my clients was a Scottish-based beer company, which didn't help the situation either. For me, Scottish was like a completely foreign language, so I'd blush every time I had to speak over the phone and would ask for each sentence to be repeated twice. I added an evening English course to my schedule, pushing away drinks with colleagues after work.

At lunchtime I would go to the local Tesco and buy two sandwiches: egg and cress, and tuna and sweetcorn, £1.10 each, the cheapest I could find. No fruit, of course, as I used to think of it as an unnecessary luxury when money was scarce. I would eat the egg and cress sandwich for lunch and keep the other one in the fridge next to the communal milk, for dinner, in case I had to work late. Most days I did.

§

At the beginning, I spoke to my mum over Skype every day. Then once a week, and then whenever I had something significant to share, meaning months could pass before she heard my voice. Brief texts, yes. But they gradually became so factual that they felt completely impersonal.

How are you?

Fine.

Work?

Quite busy.

Make sure you eat well. Lots of fruit and vegetables.

Sure, Mum.

And always use your brain.

Need to go now; bye, Mum.

Did I ever ask her how she was feeling? I was too wrapped up in my own existence and new life to ask any questions in return. I imagined her in the blue woollen dress, waiting every evening for the phone to ring before falling asleep on the sofa, alone.

Since Ka was born, I've started calling her more often. Perhaps becoming a mother brought me closer to her. I now understand what it means to feel the urge to make yourself available for your child, no matter the time of the day, how tired you are or how depleted your personal mental state.

§

A couple of months after I joined the marketing agency, I moved out of the room in Streatham which I shared with a girl I'd met on Gumtree, and I rented a basement studio near Old Street, part of an old Victorian house split into flats, ten minutes from work. The reason I went for it was to save on public transport costs, having no idea that the same money would get me a decent one-bedroom flat above ground the minute I moved out of zones one and two.

But the studio bewitched me. From the moment I saw the place, empty and clean, I decided to keep it sparse. I couldn't afford a bigger place, so I had to find a way to feel comfortable within its area of sixteen square metres.

I had a hammock in one corner hanging from the ceiling, which the owner was kind enough to allow and also to put up. I was using it as a bed, sofa and somewhere to swing my tired legs while my memories were oscillating rhythmically between now and back then, between thoughts I should keep and those I should let go. A couple of piles of books leaned against the wall, the ones I couldn't find in the local library or those which contained passages I wanted the freedom to underline so I could go back to them again and again.

My clothes (I didn't have many) as well as a couple of leather handbags, a pillow and a blanket, were all stored in a built-in wardrobe. In there I also kept a wooden box with an assortment of earrings: a pair from each city I've ever been to, like those fridge magnets people like to collect as memorabilia. A few aromatic candles on the floor, for decoration, meditation and dim lighting, were placed next to the African djembe someone got for me from Camden Market. I didn't play the djembe, but loved the rhythm it created and often invited friends over who could play it for me. Cushions in bright geometrical patterns on the floor, arranged in no particular order, added colour to the stark whiteness of the space. The only items I bought myself were a dark blue floor lamp, arching over the hammock, and a couple of paintings: an oil canvas of three African women carrying big water cans on their heads, and a fabric collage of a crying Russian doll, which I found strange and decided to keep until I worked out why a Russian doll would cry.

In the kitchen, separated from the rest of the room by a breakfast bar, were a stove, a washing machine and a high cupboard with a few plates, bowls, cups, glasses, and a pot. There were a few other essentials I kept in my backpack: a laptop, a camera, a notebook.

And that was all. I was living my clutter-free life in a clutter-free flat, not willing to create a sense of belonging to a place or an object. It gave me space to think, to enjoy myself, simply to be. Space to feel free. To everyone visiting for the first time it seemed empty but to me it was rich, and also enriching. I was the same with people: only borrowing their time and affection when needed, staying away from nostalgia, from attachment and deep feelings.

If I wasn't working at the weekend, I'd give myself in to a lazy morning with a cup of coffee and a captivating book from the library. The coffee aroma would mingle with the smell of damp. It was the first thing I had to get used to, soon paired with the darkness in the room and the shadows creeping up the walls, hiding in corners and leaving behind a sense of constant dusk.

I would read for hours in the hammock without noticing the day had halved. Then I would go out for a walk and, on the way back, buy a few things from the Turkish shop further down the street. The guy always welcomed me with a big smile on his bearded face.

– *Marhaba*. He would show his gleaming teeth.

– Are you Turkish too? an old lady asked me once while touching the figs one by one.

– No. Bulgarian.

– Then how come you understand Ali? Did you study Turkish at school?

– No. It's a leftover from our collective memory, I suppose.

She didn't understand and moved towards the pears, again touching every single one of them with her fingers, crooked with arthritis.

On my way back to the flat, I thought of this shared past. Strangely, that same past would segregate us, Bulgarians, and the Turkish people back home, while here, in this foreign country, it brings us closer.

§

My neighbours from the flat above mine were a guy named Kyron and his daughter, a lovely curly-haired girl aged seven or eight. Kyron had moved to London ten years ago, met a woman, fallen crazy in love, got married, had a baby girl. Everything seemed to be great until one day he found a note on the fridge: 'Sorry, I'm leaving'. Just that. No explanations, no goodbyes, no mention of the child. Kyron decided to raise the girl himself; after all, there wasn't any other choice left for him. He told me this story when we first met, right on the stairs in front of the house, when I was moving in. I guess he was used to telling it so many times, the words didn't mean much to him any more, as if over time they had lost their power, like a scent slowly fading away.

Kyron would often stop by my flat and, being new in town, I didn't mind. He would bring me home-made cookies, he would cook dinner for me on a Friday night when I'd been working late and would even slip a note under my door, wishing me goodnight. Occasionally, I would offer to babysit on a Saturday evening, so he could go out on a date. This didn't happen often, so I didn't mind.

Sometimes, he would bring a bottle of wine. He would come in, pour the wine in two glasses, light the candles and peel off my dress. He would scoop my face into his palms and sprinkle an invisible line of kisses starting from just under my fringe, sliding down my nose, my wanting lips, my neck. His fingers would play with the strands of my hair, following their length down to my bare shoulders where they ended. I would never get to taste the wine. I loved examining his face in which different cultures entwined, telling me stories about worlds I didn't know. I found it enigmatic without understanding then the convoluted narrative his skin colour carried. We would make love on the floor, our bodies merging, glowing, his dreads, normally wrapped in a high bun, spilling gently over my face like a waterfall, the contrast between our skins blurring. Then we'd dress up and sit on the stairs in front of the house, chain-smoking and chatting.

I loved our conversations in those moments, imbued with the stillness of the night. He was a freelance film-maker, running classes at a not-for-profit organization helping children from disadvantaged communities to learn how to produce films, and supplemented this income with filming weddings at weekends, if the clients didn't mind him bringing the child along. This gave him the flexibility he needed to look after his daughter, do the school run and pay the bills.

Kyron was now working on his own project, a documentary exploring the connection between people and cities. He was interested in contrasts: his words. He would film people sleeping rough in front of skyscrapers in the city, others queuing for a free meal in the churchyards close to big supermarkets' bins with out-of-date food. He was influenced by Sebastião Salgado, who, through stunning, breathtaking landscapes and portrait photos, would highlight social issues like inequality and human suffering. Salgado was called controversial, labelled as a poverty porn photographer, but Kyron had a very strong opinion about this.

– Someone has to start the conversation, you know, he explained to me once. To show things other people might not see at first, or might have never come across. We need to expose the truth.

But he would also film solutions, as he liked to say. Like kids of all colours playing football together. Or a family, in fact a family that lived on our street, adopting three refugee siblings despite having two kids of their own.

Some evenings he would come to my place with his camera and take pictures of me: of my olive-skinned face, my arms crossed across my tiny breasts, my bony back, revealing the shadows in my naked body, a subtle glimpse of what the imagination might reveal. These improvised photo sessions would prolong the moment, make me impatient, infuse the night with desire. He made a promise never to show the photos to anyone, a promise forged between our naked bodies.

There were times when he stayed and we had dinner together, stuffing our mouths as if we hadn't eaten for ages. His knees would occasionally knock against mine, which sent electrical waves through my body every time. He would clear up and wash the plates in the sink while I sat behind him, taking in the view of his broad shoulders.

my first boyfriend was broad-shouldered and narrow-minded; I was fourteen or fifteen and defined 'boyfriend' as someone with whom to hang out, hold hands and share a taste in music; to walk down the street with, his fingers laced into mine, our palms sweating, firstly because I was shy, and secondly out of fear that my father might see us and yell at me for not going straight back home after school; I knew my father's palms well; they would cleave firmly to my cheek the moment I opened the front door, but I was trying to put aside this thought; I let myself linger instead in the present for as long as possible, enjoying the softness of the evening and inhaling my boyfriend's scent mixed with the smell of roasted shrimps

when my boyfriend stopped holding my hand I realized he no longer cared for me and I started searching for another boy with the same musical taste and a different fragrance; I craved their attention but didn't want to be reminded of the previous rejection

For my twenty-fifth birthday I gathered friends together in the communal back garden of the house, including Kyron and his daughter. He was happy; he took on the role of host and cooked his succulent dishes, fired up the barbecue, surprised me with a home-made cake. I put on a white top and jeans, brought out the alcohol and my red-painted lips, and was ready to embrace the evening.

My friends started to arrive and I eased myself into the crowd, drinking and chatting. I noticed how they studied Kyron: the guys with curiosity, the women with leering eyes. I looked at him too, from afar. He seemed relaxed and chatty, trying to catch a glimpse of me in between conversations with other people, laughing.

As darkness settled over the garden, we lit the firepit and sat around in a circle. The deal I'd struck was that everyone should bring a musical instrument they could play. We followed each other, our different abilities creating a mesmerizing infusion of rhythm and sound. I brought out my djembe, pretending I knew what I was doing.

It was late; Kyron's daughter was tired, so he went upstairs to put her to sleep, then came back and sat right next to me. He touched my hand, my bare arm. I could feel his presence next to my face, sliding down my body, unsure if the warmth was him or the alcohol, and I closed my eyes.

– Do you know what djembe means? It comes from the saying *Anke djé, anke bé*, which translates as 'everyone gather together in peace', he whispered, his soft lips almost touching my ear.

Before finishing the sentence, he grabbed the djembe from my hands and started playing it.

I sensed my friends hovering at the edge of my vision, all eyes.

– You seem such a lovely couple, a friend said before leaving.

I wanted to reply that it wasn't what she was thinking, but I said nothing and smiled, repressing the urge to explain.

When everyone had left and it was just the two of us in the garden, smoking a joint and looking at the sky, he gave me a gift, a handmade necklace and a card with a message inside: 'Loving is creating. Happy birthday!' He buried his fingers in my sun-lightened hair, inhaling my skin. It was a moment that stretched into the night and felt like home, and true. We didn't make love. Somehow, his presence was enough.

Going to bed later that night, I felt light for the first time in a long time, not quite understanding why.

§

Yesterday I attended Ka's parents' evening at the nursery, a pricey but highly recommended Montessori one, named Five Little Ducklings. The teacher was new and looked disappointed.

– No offence, but I thought Ka's mother was attending this meeting, she said to me politely while taking her glasses off.

– No offence taken; I *am* Ka's mother, I replied, forcing myself to smile.

A puzzled look followed and a brief apology before she took me through Ka's report, explaining what activities she enjoyed most. Somehow she was still unable to accept that this woman, olive-skinned, with an Eastern European accent, could possibly be the parent of the white-skinned, very blonde and very English-sounding little girl.

For the first time I was able to see the deep chasm between me and my daughter, the way we were seen by people we greeted every day. Her father's Britishness had overpowered my otherness in her. I should be grateful to him for this as, living in this country, it worked to our child's benefit. But I wasn't.

What if, I thought, one day we went back to my homeland? Would her Britishness make her better off, or worse, different? Would she be able to ease into that other place, surrounded by the local people? You change location and all the rules of *local* and *other* change, of *acceptance* and *exclusion*.

I thanked the teacher, put the report in my handbag and left. I didn't ask a single question, in order not to widen the abyss, not to make my daughter ashamed of her mother's otherness.

§

– How are you feeling today?
    – Out of my place, whatever that place is. Different.
    – What makes you feel that way?

he was playing with my hair when he broke up with me; he told me he'd kissed another girl from my class and I bit my lips so hard they bled but I didn't shed a tear; he had loved my long tresses, touching them, smelling them, burying his fingers in them while kissing me, and that had made me feel beautiful

(the long hair that symbolized my female power over him, vs the short hair that would label me un-pretty, un-girly, un-feminine)

the next morning I went to the barber and asked him to shave my head; he looked at me, puzzled, and didn't want to do it at first, but I wouldn't leave, so he had to in the end

I didn't want to be defined by my hair

I didn't want to keep anything he used to like about me, my boyfriend in year ten

I wanted to feel different

Over time, Kyron started going out on dates less often and started spending more evenings at my place after putting his child to bed. I liked it this way, or at least I didn't mind. He was kind to me, his naked brown arms were warm and soft, his breath had a delicate sweetness.

Sometimes he would come tiptoeing down, knocking on my door. If I didn't answer, he'd guess I was with someone else. He would drag his disappointment slowly up the stairs, his heavy steps would echo in my head. I would imagine him curling up in bed like a question mark, staring into the darkness. At other times I could sense him peering through the window when a man escorted me home in the small hours, in the brief moment before I sidled into my flat. He would be hiding behind the blinds when I looked up, unashamed of my face distorted by alcohol and its smudged eyeliner, but he wouldn't say anything the next day.

He started to mind the imprints of other men, the fact that I brought their sexual likes and dislikes with me, or maybe he had always minded but had remained silent, so as not to ruin things between us.

I knew he understood. He was charming, but he was a single father with no childcare options. I, on the other hand, was young, with long legs and endless opportunities. He was my midnight feast, teasing and satisfying without the guilt, and I didn't want it otherwise.

One night, while smoking on the stairs in front of the house, he kissed me, caressed my hair and said that that was the last time we were having sex. He said it was toxic for both of us and we should try to move on. As if life is linear and we live it inch by inch, leaving things behind, moving on, advancing towards something, perhaps, the end. In my mind, the geometry of life has different dimensions. I prefer to think that we gravitate around ideas, places and people; at times getting closer, at others moving apart.

I was angry with him, but I also understood. While I was living in the moment, he was planning for the future. I was afraid to let myself love him, while he was ready to give in to me. I would do anything to stay away from pain, while he had accepted that a relationship could bring both pleasure and disappointment.

I couldn't bear to be reminded of his touch, of his deep voice reverberating around me, of all the moments of intimacy we shared in the corners of the night. Leafing through the glossy magazine in the nearby hairdresser's, I pointed at a short blonde hairstyle, one that echoed from years ago.

A few weeks later I moved out of the flat.

§

On the train to work the other day, I sat opposite two women whose conversation caught my attention. One of them, sad-looking under her dark fringe, startled me the moment she started talking.

– I recently published a poetry collection on the topic of domestic abuse and childhood trauma, she said. It was therapeutic, you know, the whole experience of going back, reliving the painful events in my head, writing them down as a way to release the tension and make myself believe it was only fiction.

The other woman was visibly older than her but had the same melancholic expression on her face, almost like a stain on a tablecloth that won't come off.

– I understand, she replied. I'm sorry about you having to go through it all.

They talked a lot about their common experiences, agreed that the story repeats itself so many times and on so many levels with other children, other grown-ups like them, still haunted by the nightmares they lived through with their eyes wide open.

Later, I thought about that need for narrating the trauma; like people hurting themselves, writing on their bodies, an appeal for help, a silent scream. I've been keeping this side of me tightly locked away. The truth is, when people learn about the abuse I experienced as a child, they look at me with pity. I prefer not to say. I prefer to act normal, so they can act normal too. Every morning I leave the house, pretending everything is fine. But isn't acting normal making me schizophrenic, being two different people in one body?

It's been so long that I find it difficult now to locate my memories, as if they were all placed in boxes along with my toys and put away in the loft. When the time is right, I will climb the stairs to that loft, tiptoeing so I don't wake the ghosts of my past.

Before starting these sessions, I used to attend a few other local groups, mainly volunteer-led. One was art therapy, which was sporadic and by invitation. We were encouraged to draw or write about our life, about the traumatic experience we'd had. It was an attempt to reconstruct the past; a reality deconstructed long ago. I needed, like that woman on the train, to find another therapy, something to help me expose the wound and let it heal. I could never forget, but I could try to forgive. I had a hard time narrating my past, the period of time that had spread its tentacles like an octopus, filling the space in between my breaths. Of course, there was no expectation that whatever we wrote would be creative. And yet we already knew that the text would be read, that the past would be exposed. Or even that it *should* be exposed, so it can heal.

§

In the months after I split up with Kyron, I would binge on work, wine and men, especially men. The days and weeks merged into each other. I'd work hard during the day, then in the evening I'd sag into the creases of the city, stopping for a quick drink in a Shoreditch bar picked at random, and would end up in someone else's flat. In the morning, waking up next to a stranger, having no recollection of events past the second glass of wine, I would frantically collect the clothes I'd left strewn over the floor and close the door behind me, applying a thick layer of red lipstick on the go.

I was trying hard to convince myself that I didn't miss Kyron, that he didn't mean much to me, reciting his last words on the stairs about our toxic relationship. I couldn't forgive myself for letting him love me, and maybe for letting myself fall in love with him.

I liked it that way, being around men.

I enjoyed their attention, their gazes slipping down and up my body, their jokes made in an attempt to make me laugh, their moves, all the same and yet desirable.

I loved flirting with them, then bringing them home in the small hours, undressing in front of their thirsty eyes, dancing all night with their hands on my hips before sending them away in the morning and locking the door behind them.

I'd been rejected by my father so many times that the only thing I could do was to get even.

it was one of those summer days, easy to lose yourself in the heaviness of the heat, waiting for the night breeze to dilute the dense air

we were in the pamporovo resort in the mountains, on holiday; during the day, we took walks in the woods, filled jars with blueberries, hiked up the hills to make ourselves tired and hungry

every parent who has a fussy eater like me knows how important it is to take their child to the mountains for fresh air, close to nature; they also know the importance of getting that same child tired and hungry

the other people in the villa praised the food in the canteen; breakfast, lunch, dinner, it was all included

– just bring your appetite

the chef laughed, his big belly trembling

but I had no appetite whatsoever; even the thought of food made me want to vomit

– where is your appetite, young lady?

he asked jokingly

– did it fall into your heels?

standing in front of the slices of cheese, butter and ham, I didn't find his words funny; at a push I could force myself to try the strawberry jam in the miniature jars

each morning, when my parents tried to wake me up, I tucked my head under the pillow, hoping to avoid the forthcoming torture of eating breakfast; mum and dad got tired of it all and one day they locked me in the room and went to have breakfast without me; at first, I didn't believe they had left me alone; I was around five or six at the time; I started calling them, but no one answered; I peeped out from under the pillow; an empty room

– mama! ma–maa!

I started crying out loud in the middle of the room, barefoot, like a prisoner left on an island from which there was no escape

sometime later, the door was unlocked and my mother stepped in

– why are you crying?

– because you abandoned me and I didn't know if you would ever return

I replied, still weeping

– we didn't abandon you; we went to have a quick bite, while you were still sleeping; now stop crying and come to see what we have brought for you

and she spread in front of me the packed breakfast; some bread and a few slices of cheese, butter and ham

STOP TWO
West End Tale

–How are you feeling today?
    – I don't want to feel. It burns my body, my intestines, my mind.
    – But you have your daughter's love. Isn't that something?
    – It is something. Something that expects love in return.

§

Ka:
    – Mama, tell me a bedtime story, will you?
    – What story, baby?
    – A magical one.
    – A magical one… Let me think… Close your eyes, then, and listen.
    – Once upon a time there was a girl named Soraya who lived far, far away in a small village up in the Rodopi mountains. Her beauty was ethereal. Her eyes were the colour of the evergreen pine trees, her skin was luminous and crystalline like the morning

dew, and her long hair was black like a deep well. She used to play in meadows all day with her best friend, a boy her age called Ivan, who loved Soraya like a sister.

'Be back before dusk, never go to the lake alone and stay away from the deep shadows,' her parents said.

'Why?' Soraya asked.

'Because these are the places where the mystical *samodivi* go. They dance in the moonlight by the lake, or hide under the deep shadows. If a *samodiva* looks a man in the eyes, he becomes enchanted, captivated forever by her unearthly beauty, and if a young girl sees them, they take her away from her family and she becomes one of them.'

Soraya didn't want to trouble her parents and always came home before dark.

'Come with me, I want to show you something,' Ivan said to her once.

'Where?' Soraya asked.

'I'll take you to the top of the mountain. You can see the whole world from there. And don't worry, we'll be back before dusk,' he replied, and took her by the hand.

Soraya followed him. They crossed the river, stepping over the stones. They walked up the hills and into the deep forest. They climbed the rocks and steep cliffs, and finally reached the top of the mountain. The view was magnificent, just as Ivan had promised Soraya.

'This is the world,' he said, 'and I want to share it with you.'

And just as he closed his eyes and tried to kiss her lips, Soraya stepped on a moving stone and fell down the cliff.

'Soraya! Soraya-a-a!' Ivan shouted after her, but she kept rolling down the rocks and into the rift until he lost sight of her. He stayed there and cried for three nights and three days, and then returned to the village and told her parents what had happened...

– Ah, someone seems very tired. Night-night, sleep tight, baby.

it's new year's eve, a few minutes past midnight, and I am crouched down, meek and still in the wardrobe in our bedroom amid hanging dresses and ironed shirts; I'm biting my lips to muffle my sobs, hands pressing my ears tightly to mute the shouting coming from the other room

my five-year-old body is quivering and I can feel the heartbeats in my head, but all other body parts are numb as though I don't exist; I must not move; I shut my eyes, I make myself small, invisible, so no one can find me; then the shouting stops

one, two, three, four… I count the seconds of quietness spread over time like a chewing gum; is she still alive, I think; five, six, seven… my mind is racing; eight, nine… when I count ten, I have to leave my secret place and aim for the phone in the other room; I must call the police and tell them where we live

I know well what to do; I have rehearsed it thousands of times before; I learned our address by heart before learning how to read; I do everything automatically, as if in my sleep, without thinking at all; everything is encoded in me

I also know time is precious; there is a window of a few seconds for me to act before my dad catches me; if I can get through in time, the policemen come, they ring the bell, my father keeps us quiet in the other room, and eventually they leave

it doesn't always work; most often they think I'm playing a prank on them and hang up on me; sometimes I manage to open the door, the policemen come in, they ask questions and leave, as there is no crime yet, it's all family matters

I pause after nine and wait; nine feels forever; nine is infinity

then a bang follows and my mum's screams enter the suffocating space through the cracks of the wardrobe doors; her cry is both disturbing and comforting, a sign that my mother is alive

46

I stay put until the shouting stops, until my mother goes to the bathroom to wash her face under the ice-cold running water, until she enters the bedroom barefoot and whispers my name, as though calling a cat when it's safe for it to come out of its hiding place; I deliberate for a moment, then take a deep breath before pushing open the creaking wardrobe door; or maybe it's the other way around

she inches towards me, kneels down to my height and her arms envelop my shaking body gently; her face looks jittery, her hair is messy, her breathing is heavy but she is forcing a smile to comfort me, to make me feel safe; I know this because she does it every time; I also know we aren't safe, not yet

– c'mon, let's go, baby, quickly

she bundles up a few clothes and stuffs them into a white bin bag, then grabs my hand and guides me into the living room; my father is asleep in the armchair, snoring, intoxicated by the alcoholic halo he's breathing back into his lungs; his face, although red and sweaty, looks calm now; we cross the room tiptoeing, aware that the slightest noise could wake him up and foil our escape; I glance at his gored fist, hanging over the chair's armrest, and wonder if it's smeared with his blood or mum's

there we are, out of the flat, leaving the front door open and unlocked so as not to wake him up; it's dark in the corridor and it smells of damp; my mum is holding me tightly by the hand as we hurtle down the stairs; we stop a few floors below and knock on the door; it's quiet at first, then the door lock clicks and I see the neighbour's confused expression, staring at us from under her bouffant hair, her eyes wide open, moving between mum's pleading face, my shaking body and our half-full bin bag

– elena, who is it

her husband shouts from inside, and he joins her in the hallway

they're celebrating new year's eve at home with family; I hear the rattle of cutlery and the hum of conversation coming from the dining

47

room; the warm aroma of cooked food reminds me I haven't eaten tonight; I imagine the steak with baked potatoes and stuffed vine leaves and Russian salad, but quickly swallow my dream and remain alert

mum asks for shelter overnight; we'll leave in the morning, she says, we'll go somewhere else; she's apologetic and begging; the thing is, this neighbour is my mum's friend, but her husband is my dad's colleague; in fact, dad is his boss; he doesn't want to be seen to help us because this would be bad for his career; it will be over and they don't want that; they're making their excuses while our hope melts away like the caramel candy they offer me; then we hear a door closing upstairs and give up on the neighbours; we run down the stairs, holding hands, holding our breath

we live on the fourteenth floor and I can't count that far yet, so my heart skips a beat when we finally reach the block exit; it's freezing cold outside, we have nowhere to go, but I feel relieved; we walk into the night under occasional fireworks, mingling with people's laughter, drunken singing and excitement; it's a new year, a new beginning

or that's what I thought back then

– All kids have a father, people say.

– How do you explain to your daughter that she doesn't have a dad, people ask, expecting my answer right away.

I had two options. To leave Milo when the girl was so little she wouldn't remember but would then pursue me over the years with her persistent question, *why?* Or never to leave, to learn to put up with whatever was happening like my mother had, to feel the searing pain and do nothing, to fall apart and do nothing, to break into pieces and do nothing. To let my daughter witness all of this and still do nothing. She would want to forget it and have never known about it.

So I chose to leave. I am prepared to answer her questions when she's old enough to understand.

Until then, I will cuddle her when she cries in the middle of the night, woken by nightmares, and everything will be fine, because I know her nightmares are imaginary.

Mine were real.

§

– And Milo is Ka's father, right? Tell me about him. How did you two meet?

§

A few years after I moved here, I changed jobs. The new agency was bigger and the managing director used to say it had a flat structure, meaning people in junior roles were expected both to make decisions and to do the work. Colleagues were nice, and less sarcastic about my accent. I was slowly reclaiming my confidence as well as my evenings and weekends.

As a side project I started writing film and theatre reviews for an online art and culture magazine. This was my way of getting free tickets to events and screenings I wanted to go to anyway. The magazine didn't have a large readership at first, but with time it started to gain traction in the cultural and media space.

One of the plays I reviewed was an immersive performance in which the audience participated, shaping the narrative and changing the direction of the story. I liked the idea but also found it a bit pretentious. My thinking was that variations of the story were obviously rehearsed in advance, carefully thought through and so, whatever the audience said, the actors would revert to one of the rehearsed options. It lets you believe you have control and own the narrative, but that impression is false.

That's what I wrote in my review. The play's director read it the next day and called the magazine, asking to speak to me. He was furious. He insisted we meet and chat about either amending my review or taking it down immediately. I didn't agree at first. He changed tactics, played his cards well. Somehow, I ended up having dinner with him that same evening at an Italian restaurant, and then drinks at his place. His voice was steady and velvety and I remember finding him arrogant and patronizing, looking down on me behind his black-framed glasses from his 6'1" height. I thought it was just a pose to make me feel uncomfortable so instead of stepping back, I pushed my arguments twice as hard. I explained to him that he might want to control the audience but had no chance of controlling my review. We argued a lot, drank a lot and fucked. A lot. The sex with him was different to anything I'd experienced before. There was something feral in him. There was passion and hunger which enticed me, but there was also an overpowering feeling of smugness, and control, as if he were trying to possess me.

That night we also laughed and talked about nice things. He asked me questions and listened. He placed his hand on my leg and left it there a long time. That was Milo, with his sleek, captivating way of making me feel desired. I went there determined to smash his ego and left his flat in the morning, already willing to come back the next day.

I remained under his spell for a couple of years. If this was a result of the initial adrenaline plus the wine, multiplied by the late hour and divided by the number of lonely nights I'd had recently, it didn't matter to begin with.

The rest then followed.

§

The moment Milo and I agreed to take it slowly, we knew we had already fallen in love with each other, deeply and unconditionally. A few months later we moved in together. It didn't make sense to pay for two flats in the crazy rental market anyway. At first, awkwardness settled in, discovering the ways we inhabited space, our likes and dislikes, the everyday inconsistencies between our initial expectations and reality. It was the little things, like my obsession with tidiness and his blindness to the mess, my inability to cook and his manic obsession with healthy eating, his snoring in the middle of the night, my singing over tunes he couldn't bear. We had to adjust to one another while still discovering what living together felt like. Bit by bit, we came to appreciate the different stages of building a relationship; when to compromise, what to tolerate and what to conceal. We became a couple without losing ourselves; self-preservation was important for both of us.

Time went by, I got pregnant, and we became a family.

– She was scared but kept walking deeper and deeper into the birch forest. And just when Vasilisa was about to give up, she heard a creak and there it was, not a house but a hut, standing on gigantic chicken legs. Before Vasilisa could say a word, the hut started pirouetting around as if performing a dance, twirling and twirling until it stopped, facing the frightened little girl. Its windows looked like eyes and the lock of the front door was full of teeth. Then it opened. Vasilisa had to be brave and walk in; she knew that this was the only way to save her dad. The moment she stepped inside, the door closed with a bang and there she was, Baba Yaga, standing right in front of Vasilisa. She was old, and skinny and ugly, with a huge hooked nose and long iron teeth.

– 'Well, well, well, let's see what we've got for dinner!'

– Mama, why is Baba Yaga living alone so deep in the forest?

– I don't know, Ka. Perhaps she doesn't want to be found.

– But then, if no children go there, she will starve and die.

– That's true. Maybe she will starve. You know this is just a tale, right? It's not really true.

– I know, I know. But how come Baba Yaga lives in the forest alone? Why doesn't she have children of her own?

– Well, some women don't want to have kids.

– And you? Have you always loved me, Mama?

§

– How are you feeling today?

– Same as yesterday.

– I like your dress.

– Thanks, but I'm not here to talk about dresses.

– OK, I see. Let's play a little association game then, shall we?

– What do you mean?

– We'll use a word you mention for a prompt. You'll tell me a story that first comes to your mind.

– OK, whatever. What's the first one then?

– Dress.

mum bought a new dress and was happy for a while

woollen, winter dress, dark blue

the neckline was shaped like a glass of wine; the dress had embroidery and a knitted belt and stopped a few inches above her knees; she had pretty legs, and hands, and hair, and face; she put the dress on and did a pirouette in front of the mirror; when dad came back from work and saw her all smiling and happy, his face turned red

– you want men to turn after you on the street, huh?

I heard him saying

then the shouting muffled his words; the beating lasted all night; all night I stayed up in my room, barefoot, frightened, only six, praying my mum would be alive in the morning

she was

I found her on the floor, still wearing the dress, blue mixed with red; I saw the sadness flowing from her eyes and turning into a puddle; the marks on her face remained for days; they were the same blue as the new dress

The night was long and my body was restless. First thing the next morning I went to the pharmacy for a pregnancy test. Impatient, I entered the coffee shop a few metres down the street, stepped into the bathroom and locked the door behind me. I held the stick under the stream of urine, my hands trembling, then I got up, tucked the vest into my jeans and waited. After a while, two clear lines appeared. I flicked the stick and looked again, as if trying to shake off the extra line.

The streets were waking up and filling with people rushing to work, their chatter overwhelming my brain. I felt lost and an urge to hide away overtook me. I called my boss and said I had a stomach bug. Then I ran home, locked myself in the bathroom and vomited.

§

– Milo, I'm pregnant.

I said those words while applying a layer of deep red lipstick with a confident gesture in front of the mirror, minutes before leaving for work. In the reflection I saw his eyes getting wider and wider, as though they would eventually take up his whole face.

– Are you sure?

His high-pitched voice irritated me.

– Of course I'm sure! I took a test yesterday.

– But how is it even possible? Aren't you on the pill?

– I am. I don't know. I must have missed a dose. Remember Jenny's birthday party three weeks ago, when we got really drunk? I can't remember if I took it the next morning, my head was still hurting.

He approached me slowly, encircled my waist with his hands as though defending me from a blow, and kissed my neck tenderly. I cringed and pushed him away curtly; his unshaven face left a red mark on my skin.

– We had a great time that night. One to remember, don't you think?

His attempt to joke offended me.

– Don't you get it, Milo? I'm not ready for this. I'm not even sure if I want to become a mother!

– Ever?

– Ever!

– What are you planning to do then?

– You mean you wouldn't mind if I...

I left the question dangling. He remained silent, sliding his glaze away from me. He didn't try to hug me again, just stepped into his shoes and left.

The second person singular in his question took me aback. There was no *we* involved, but at the same time I had his permission to act as I liked. The truth was, neither of us was ready to become a parent, and I was sure that thought would be playing on his mind as well as mine. But he contained himself and somehow adjusted to the idea over the next days. Knowing his busy schedule, often touring out of the city for weeks on end, I knew full well that the responsibility of raising a child would weigh heavily on me. But it wasn't just that. Questions and doubts reverberated in my head, spinning around, making me feel dizzy.

My reflection was still there, looking at me from the mirror, silently awaiting my decision. I contoured my eyes with a black pencil, applied dark grey eyeshadow with a brush to create a contrast with the khaki colour of my eyes, highlighted my cheekbones with blusher. There we go, ready to face what was about to follow.

After years of practice, I was confident I could do it with my eyes closed. Five minutes a day was all I needed to apply the thin protective membrane between me and the outside world, and with it the reassurance that I could restrain myself within my own contours, and vouchsafe to others only what they needed to see. A slightly different face, full of colour and life, both mine and not, the face that people would be happy to see.

Sometimes I wonder what Milo saw in this face. I wonder whether he still remembers what drew him towards me that first time at his flat, when his grey-blue eyes pinned mine. When did he decide to stay with me?

The following evenings were tense and uneasy for both of us. We could both see our feelings crumbling on the floor in front of us, both of us unwilling to make an effort and pick them up. He was trying to come to terms with impending parenthood, while I was already planning to erase the child from my imminent future without completely obliterating my relationship with Milo.

The words, unspoken, dug deep holes in me; the wind hid in them and played with my hollow body all night.

on the last day of the summer holiday just before starting year seven, I bought a red lipstick from the corner shop with the change from buying bread and milk that I'd been allowed to keep as a reward for doing the daily shopping

I was thirteen, pale and curious; the lipstick was cheap and shiny; back home, I went into my bedroom, shut the door and twisted the lipstick up carefully; its warm smell and smooth shape mesmerized me; I tried it on in front of the mirror

just then I heard my dad's voice; what was he doing home so early?

I attempted to wipe my lips with the back of my hand; I tore a page from the book I was reading and wrapped it round the lipstick in panic then tucked it quickly under the pillow; too late: my dad entered the room and, noticing my grotesque face, started laughing; his laugh became grotesque too, barking like a dog, a big angry dog

– give me that thing, girl!

his eyes glinted with anger

– you look like a prostitute! don't you dare put red lipstick on ever again!

but isn't the forbidden what we long for most?

– Mama, what happened to Ivan after Soraya fell down the cliff?

– Years passed by. Ivan grew into a handsome young man and became a shepherd. He used to play his *kaval*, a special pipe that made the birds stop their songs and listen. His music was magical.

'Boy, your *kaval* will wake the *samodivi*,' the village people used to say.

One day, while Ivan was resting under the deep shadow, playing his *kaval*, he heard a song. A sweet woman's voice, light like the wind, dulcet like the stream. The moment he stopped playing, the melody ceased too. When he started playing the *kaval*, the voice followed again. Ivan played for hours, until it got dark. His lips were sore and his fingers blistered, but he kept playing, not feeling tired, giving himself up to the sweetness of the mystical voice.

–When night fell and the moon saw its reflection in the limpid waters of the lake, a dozen beautiful women approached, all barefoot, dressed in long white shirts which were tightened by rainbow belts. The women held hands and started dancing in a circle, their feet barely touching the ground, their white faces shining like the moon, their laughter echoing in the rocks. Ivan couldn't move. Mesmerized by the sight, he stayed quietly behind a tree, gazing at the women. He had heard about the *samodivi*, but like most people didn't believe they existed. One of them stopped dancing, turned towards him and looked right into his eyes.

–'Soraya,' he whispered, rubbing his eyes. 'Is that you?'

§

Milo, one evening over dinner:
   – Will you marry me?

59

– What? Why?
– Because I love you. And because we're going to have a baby.
– Maybe we are. But I still won't marry you. What's the point?
– What do you mean *maybe*?

it was the beginning of september, a week before the start of the new school year; mum and dad had arrived the night before to take me back to the city after a summer-long holiday with my grandparents

after breakfast, I put on my new white dress and mum plaited my hair; we all got into the old moskvitch, my grandparents and us, no room to breathe, and drove off

when we got there, the band, a roma orchestra, had already started playing, and a crowd of spectators from the neighbourhood had gathered in front of the block; we passed through the crowd and took the stairs up to the third floor; the staircase was wet as if it had just been cleaned, and it smelled of damp and mould

we were from the bride's side, so my mother and I stepped into the girl's bedroom, where at least a dozen women were already fussing around; one of them was styling the bride's hair and was nesting a pearl tiara, another one was applying the light-pink lipstick, and a third one was fixing lace over the satin lining of the layered dress

I was mesmerized by the sparkling whiteness of this dress, as if it was sprinkled with beads, when someone started banging; at that second the women rushed towards the door, pressing against it firmly with their bodies, not allowing whoever was on the other side to open it

– we've come for the bride

the men were roaring and jostling, forcing the door and opening it a centimetre with each push

for a brief moment my eyes met the bride's; I must have looked terrified, because she approached me, gently took my face in her palms and whispered in my ear

– don't be alarmed; this is just a ritual; they're my fiancé's brothers and cousins; they've come to steal me, but they won't steal me for real; we're all just pretending, ok?

*then she took off her shoe nimbly and passed it to one of the women;
the bustle and the flurry intensified, and when the door opened slightly
with the next bang, the woman managed to squeeze the shoe through
then bolted the door again*

*– if you want the bride, you have to pay the ransom
she shouted*

*– fill the shoe with money, so it will fit better; it's too wide for her
now; but don't put coins in, or her feet will get blisters*

*in less than a minute the shoe was returned, stuffed with notes
– it's still too big; put some more in*

*the woman pushed the shoe back to the men, crowded on the other side
– does it fit now?
the men asked*

– it does

the bride replied this time, and winked at me

*clapping and cheering followed from both sides of the door, and the
orchestra started banging their davul drums again; the bride's mother
kissed her daughter on the forehead, tears in her eyes, and put a veil
over her face; at that moment the women opened the door wide; the
bride stepped out of her room and walked down the stairs, followed
by the relatives and friends, all cheering and clapping to the roma
orchestra's rhythm*

*on the street, in front of the building, the fiancé was waiting for the
bride in a white lada decorated with flowers and balloons*

*that same evening I was sitting on my dad's lap, my body shaking
from the nervous tic in his right leg; I was too scared to ask him to let
me get off; I knew that I shouldn't make him angry when he was drunk;
it was just me and him in the car, parked on the street, outside the
restaurant; I looked at the people clustered before our eyes; the men,
in suits and unbuttoned shirts half-tucked into their trousers, were
shouting one over another, and the women, in their beautiful dresses
with their backcombed hairstyles, were fussing around*

I noticed my granddad in the crowd; he seemed upset; I saw him gesticulating, explaining something nervously; I couldn't hear what he was saying but I sensed his distress

– go find your mother

my dad's voice took me aback

I looked at him; his nose was disfigured, his upper lip was split

great, I can finally get away from here, I thought, and just before I managed to jump out of the car, his hand stopped me

– wait; no, you'll stay here with me; you'll be my hostage

he said it as a joke, but that was precisely how I felt

my granddad was apologizing to the guests for my dad destroying the party; my mum was probably crying again in the restaurant's toilet while my grandma banged on the door, telling her that her husband's drunkenness and violence wasn't her fault; and me, I was still sitting on my father's knees observing all this palaver as if in slow motion, praying it was only a dream, only a nightmare which would stop the minute I woke

but it wasn't a dream

that night, I sat on the bed for hours looking through the darkness, my eyes sore from crying, whispering for him

to stop hurting her

to leave her alone

to keep her alive

I didn't want to cover my ears with my hands, afraid my mother might stop screaming without me noticing, that she might stop breathing without me noticing; her screams were the proof she was still alive, each and every night

I fell asleep in the morning, when the screaming from the kitchen had died down

I heard my mother's quiet steps when she entered the room and went to bed; then I heard her hushed weeping and I wished I could comfort her, as if she were the child and I were the mother; I wished

I could hug her, but I didn't dare touch her body, tender with pain; her hair looked tangled from being pulled, her voice sounded hoarse from her pleas to make it stop

I hated him; with rage trapped under my skin I fell asleep at last and dreamed of the ocean, dreamed I was a fish that could catch the current and drift into the deep blue

– How are you feeling today?

– Full. Full of dirty, poisoned air. Pregnant with my own toxic thoughts.

§

I couldn't accept that chance had decided for me. A missed pill after drunken sex. I wasn't feeling pregnant with a baby but pregnant with a burden, with fear of my own history chasing me and repeating itself. I knew those thoughts were poisonous. I had to find a way to distinguish my feelings for the unborn baby from my feelings of insecurity, hoarded deep inside me.

You can't say I didn't try. My body was my enemy and my thoughts about killing the baby were an attempt to save her. I took a deep breath, held it, and exhaled. I closed my eyes and began to descend in a spiral towards the core of my womb. I was right there. The darkness was impenetrable, but the chaos was turning itself into order and life was starting to emerge. Through the umbilical cord I injected the embryo with my aggression accumulated over the years. Within its DNA I entwined my own fear of rejection; the amniotic fluid was now filled up with my guilt, which got absorbed by the embryo, the permeable membranes received it hospitably, it mixed with the baby's cells and with the cells of all other children coming into this world.

I put my body into self-destruct cigarette-and-alcohol mode in the hope of drowning my maternal instincts before they started to emerge, and the embryo before its heart started to beat. Every hour I would run to the toilet and stare at the water wishing to see my menstrual flow there, the baby's remains and the beginning of the end. But the water in the toilet remained clear, as if this creature had decided to hold on tightly to me in spite of my attempts to unplug it from the placenta and to flush away its short existence. Was I a murderer? My conscience wouldn't dare say anything, it kept quiet and just looked at me, noticing me pushing my tummy hard, praying this being would somehow detach from me, would leave me alone, would never expect my love and worry.

I was not sure what was worse: to remove it, or to give birth and fill up its life with my guilt.

As a grown woman, working full-time, my savings would be enough to cover the procedure. I fell asleep finding reassurance in that thought, my confidence bolstered already.

§

I had done it before, years ago. I was still at uni when I aborted a future family I could have had with the man I was dating at the time, a tall guy, seven years older than me, with tawny hair and cold eyes. I was still under the spell of my own conception, deeply engraved into my subconscious, the guilt that my coming into this world had caused a hurricane of unhappiness for my mother, the fear embroidering my perception, knitting layers around it, wrapping it in a cocoon.

When the air was crisp and my thoughts were acute one winter morning after I had missed my period by over a week, I called a private clinic. They booked me in for the next day, asking to bring in a sum that equalled all my savings.

I vividly remember my shock at the gynaecologist's words, legs spread, body shaking.

– You're pregnant.

And then a question followed:

– What are we going to do about it?

66

The question implied that something needed to be done about it. Also, that there was a *we* involved. My post-communist society didn't want young mothers in need of financial support; it expected girls to study, then to work. This paradigm would change just a few years later, but at that moment I had to follow the rules. The idea had already taken root; there was nothing left for me to decide. Without calling anyone, I hurried back to my room in halls, took the money I had squirrelled at the bottom of my jewellery box, the *just in case money* I kept there, and rushed back to the surgery. The doctor was waiting for me. We took a taxi to a private hospital in the suburbs, where he performed the operation. It happened quickly.

The anaesthetic took over my body, my mind. In that delirium I felt something being scraped from me, a deep, prolonged feeling of scratching. Chatter and laughter reached me as if the voices were coming from underwater; cold, distant, subtle.

– How did it go? I asked when I woke a few hours later.

– We removed it successfully. It's all done now, the doctor replied.

– What was it, a boy or a girl?

– Impossible to say; it's too early.

– I don't want to know any more.

– There is no more.

I paid and left a couple of hours later. I called a taxi but didn't have enough cash on me, so the driver stopped a few streets away and I walked to the campus.

Back in my room, I rested for a while, then cooked dinner before my boyfriend knocked on the door. My room-mate was rarely home, making the place a comfortable nest for us to see each other undisturbed. I greeted my boyfriend; he placed a kiss on my forehead as though checking if I was ill. I told him briefly what I had done. He approved. He said I was too young, his job was too unstable. The truth was that he was married, but he didn't tell me that. I found out a year later when his wife turned up on my doorstep. She had grown suspicious after seeing a message from me, and the next day had followed him to my place. Regardless, it was true I needed to focus on my study.

We sat at the table, but I could barely touch my meal. It was difficult for me to swallow the food. The unborn child was lying between us on the dining table. It was my body, my life. But was it a murder? He didn't ask how I felt. I didn't want to feel.

We ate the potato stew in silence, but I didn't finish mine. The pungent smell of marjoram and garlic in the dish reminded me of my mother's meals. The food on my plate went cold, but I couldn't throw it away.

I couldn't make myself throw anything away any more.

when she saw me sitting on the steps outside our block of flats, my head buried between my knees, my neighbour dropped her shopping bag aside, bent over me and shoved her wrinkled face so close to mine that I could smell the garlic she'd eaten the previous night

I knew she was one of them, one of those people whispering in the lift or in the queue in the supermarket things like 'poor children', or 'those kids have no childhood'; my mother pretended not to hear them; when we were present they acted as if we didn't exist

the woman grabbed my arms with both hands and said that fish-bowls bring bad luck; she said just that, then slid through the front door and into her flat

I took her words with the naivety of someone desperate to try everything; she must have heard about our bad luck, I thought, she must be willing to help; I needed to find a way to get rid of the bowl

I planned it for two whole days; my revenge, my first crime

on the third day, the moment I came back from school, I didn't warm up my meal as usual and I didn't do my homework; instead, I opened the newspaper and placed it on the dining table; I spent the next few minutes looking at the fish in the bowl, indulging in the thought of sacrificing them to evil forces, then rolled up my sleeves and dunked my fist into the water

I grabbed the little ones first, felt their slippery bodies, then squeezed them between my fingers and dropped what was left of them back into the bowl; the rest of the fish were spiralling around in panic, hitting the glass walls but then, realizing perhaps that there was no way to escape, swimming back to the other side, to the bottom of the aquarium, hiding between the stones and seashells

no, there was no escape; both the fish and I knew this was the only possible solution; I started catching the bigger ones and, one by one, placed them on the newspaper; then, using a kitchen knife, I halved them in one precise move; they flapped their tails right up to the point when the blade touched their slippery bodies; that was it; I left them lying soulless over yesterday's news

afterwards, I warmed up the meal on the stove, had lunch, did my homework and almost completely forgot about the whole thing until my father came back from work; it took him about a minute to see the aftermath of my afternoon pursuit and rush into my room

– what happened to the fish?

he was livid

– whatever was supposed to happen, happened, dad

I replied as if none of it was any of his business

he looked at me intensely; I was expecting him to pummel me any minute, but instead he closed the door, and that was the last time we ever talked about the fish

There were moments like this when he would come back from work not drunk, when he would somehow hear my thoughts and regret everything he was doing to us. Perhaps he too was secretly planning to get rid of the aquarium to kill the bad luck.

§

While carrying my sister, my mother was reading *Shōgun*, so my sister's eyes are slightly Asian-looking. When she was pregnant with me, she added parsley to each meal, so my eyes turned green. That's what she told me; I don't know if she believed any of it herself.

While I was pregnant with Ka, although I'm not superstitious, I followed strictly all the diets and beliefs I'd heard. I would have a bite from everything that I fancied eating, so no marks would appear on my child's body as a sign of my unfulfilled desire. I even gave in to a McDonald's double cheeseburger. It would be devastating if I marked my child with the big M, I thought.

I was vomiting all night

– it's probably from the eggs you ate for dinner, they must have been spoiled

my mother said, then made me some rice water and spearmint tea

she asked me to take a few small sips from the big ceramic mug, but I was sulking and vomiting again until nothing remained in my stomach; then I snuggled up to this emptiness and fell asleep

a week later my mother started vomiting; my father, instead of making her spearmint tea, turned to me with a smile and said

– you'll soon have a brother or sister

that's what he said, a brother or sister

soon

During my whole pregnancy, there was a dull pain in my head just above my left ear. It was sleeping in its nest, that's how I used to imagine it, sleeping there like a magpie, and every time I went to bed with wet hair, it left its nest and started pecking my head, eating my brain, not letting me think straight.

My grandma used to say that I should keep my feet dry as the cold gets into the body from the feet up, but for me it was from the head down. The pain rankled inside, scratched my temples, flapped its wings behind my forehead, it covered my eyes with blackness. I started feeling sick and dizzy, tried to vomit and sometimes even succeeded, but the pain kept its place there, nestling, laughing at me.

The midwife asked me how I was feeling and I said *fine*, then lay on the couch. She rubbed her hands to warm them up and started examining my bump, touching it gently, spreading some cold jelly all over it so she could see the baby on the ultrasound. There, on the small screen, I started to recognize the contours of the baby that existed as part of me and at the same time was living its own separate life.

When it was all over, I wiped the slime from my belly with the blue paper and got up quickly. I was afraid that if I stayed a bit longer, she might discover something wrong; that she might move the ultrasound towards my head and see my pain.

she'd been handwashing the clothes in the bathroom for over an hour, I remember, and my anxiety was growing and growing like raindrops on a leaf, ready to fall; several times I tried to get in, but she ordered me to stay away

writhing on the floor in front of the door, head crammed into my knees, I could hear her sobbing; it was the time of severe economic crisis, the time of savings; when there was water, there was no electricity, and vice versa; mum was hurrying to wash while the water was on, but she had never been in the bathroom for so long, so I knew something wasn't right

my father got home from work and when I told him that mum had been in the bathroom for over an hour, he rushed in without even taking off his shoes; he opened the door and I tried to peek inside from behind his back; the candle had burned and mum stood in the dark, bent over the sink, breathing heavily

she said something to my dad which I couldn't hear; he hugged her around the waist and helped her sit on the armchair in the living room; he grabbed her slippers, nightgown and her toiletries, and shoved them into the bag, which had been waiting in the hallway for days

– what are you putting in this bag?

I had asked my mother as she was packing it two weeks ago

– baby nappies, clothes, a blanket

she replied

– is the baby coming now?

I asked, my eyes wide open

– not right now but soon; I will let you know when the time comes

that was two weeks ago

– mum, has the time come?

my voice trembled but she just glanced over me, groaned again and I knew dad helped her put on her coat and boots; it was more than an hour until the electricity would be on again, and there was no time to waste, so dad held mum gently and we all started creeping down the stairs

mum was leaning against the railing, trying hard not to groan; dad was doing a bad job of motivating her to take another step; from the tenth floor onwards he told her we were nearly there, and so, in tiny steps and huge efforts, the three of us walked down to the ground floor and got in the car

when we arrived at the hospital, mum kissed me and told me to be a good girl while she was away; only then did I realize that I would have to stay alone with my father for days

– when will you come back?

I cried

– soon

she replied, and sank into the ward

a few days later, she walked out of that same door, this time holding a baby in her arms

– meet your little sister

she said, leaning forward so I could have a look at her face

my sister appeared on a cold but sunny november day; in the car I couldn't take my eyes off this cute little creature that was quietly entering my life

would we share the fear the same way we would be sharing our bedroom?

In the early weeks of my pregnancy I used to cry often and go to the toilet frequently. I would lock myself in the bathroom and pour everything out. I remember feeling relaxed and lighter then, despite the few kilograms I'd gained.

I was patiently waiting for the baby to come out of me, just like the tears and the urine. How wrong was that, praying to lose my baby? Was I some weirdo, or a witch?

§

On a warm and beautiful day, a friend and I were walking down the street; the sun's rays beamed through my eyelashes and embroidered my face like lace. We passed a second-hand shop with big SALE signs on the windows; a fish and chip shop with a crowd of teenage schoolkids gathered outside, some queuing, others already digging into the fried drumsticks with oily fingers; a flower shop with dark blue irises, white and yellow daisies, and red gerberas in big plastic buckets placed on the pavement; and then a local bakery with inviting glazed doughnuts, mini croissants and cupcakes with thick chocolate icing on top that tempted my eyes and made my stomach rumble.

We stepped into the bakery and I left with a big pack of jam-filled doughnuts, offered them to my friend, gobbled one up and shoved the rest into my tote bag for later. My fingers sank into the dough, soft and gooey; its sweetness gave me pleasure and I closed my eyes for a moment. The raspberry jam squeezed through my teeth and dropped onto my yellow shirt, bright red. I attempted to clean it with a tissue, which made things worse so I gave up, aware it would stain and ruin my top but determined not to let it spoil my day.

I looked up to the balconies of the buildings, studying the laundry hanging there to dry. There is something deeply intimate in this act. You notice people's clothes, their dresses, shirts, socks, all sorts of underwear, hanging out freely to the stranger's gaze. There is pleasure, some sort of voyeuristic satisfaction in this act. You're free to look up shamelessly and imagine their owners' bodies, their lives.

One of them displayed baby blankets and clothes; pure white short-sleeved bodies and suits. My friend somehow caught my thoughts.

– We've been trying for years, you know, she started. Nothing. We tried everything, whatever the doctors said, whatever advice people gave us, alternative therapies, we've done it all. Nothing. Our last hope is IVF, but going private is too expensive and we simply can't afford it. We've been on the NHS waiting list for months, but God knows when our turn will come up. And even then, there's no guarantee things will happen for us. You can't possibly imagine the vast amount of money we've paid already for doctors, private clinics, special diets... But I'd pay for them again if I knew there was even a slight chance. This child is everything I've ever dreamed of, you know? For me, there's nothing more important in life than becoming a mother. You're so lucky.

Immediately I regretted telling her about the baby. I felt somewhat guilty because I was pregnant and she wasn't. That things had happened so easily with me, so quickly, too quickly in fact, and without me even planning them. At the same time, I rebelled against this common thinking that every woman dreams of being a mother, the only choice mankind has given her without the right to object. While my friend suffered deeply with each of her monthly periods, I was petrified at the thought of the kind of motherhood that the world expected of me.

As a teenager, every time I came home late, I'd be cautioned about an impending pregnancy hiding around the dark corner, as if getting pregnant was the evil enemy of young women that would obliterate their future, their career, their life. Just a few fragile years later, this whole preconception dissolves and a new one is born, the assumption that the acme of being a woman is to become a mother. I was feeling as though all eyes were on me, expecting me to enjoy my pregnancy.

– Only the witches remain childless, my friend continued. You know, only Baba Yaga has no children, but she eats other people's kids.

She took pride in her joke.

Suddenly, I felt guilty for being blessed with a baby when my friend wasn't. I imagined myself in a hut resting on chicken legs while waiting for the water in the big pot to boil. The thought scared me and I changed the topic.

once in the nursery I fell from a climbing frame and broke my arm;
the teacher phoned my mother, who phoned my father, and they both
came to pick me up; they took me to the hospital; the doctor did an
x-ray, then grabbed my hand firmly and put the broken bone in place
   – all done; you're such a hero; everything will be fine; and you
know what people say, broken things bring good luck
   then he carefully put a plaster cast on my arm and sent us home
   one night, my dad broke my mum's rib; the doctor did an x-ray,
but there was no way to fix the broken rib or to plaster it
   – broken things bring good luck; everything will be fine
   I kept repeating to myself like a mantra

mum stayed in bed for weeks
   there is a power, like an invisible umbilical cord that still connects
us, my mother and me

The baby was growing inside me, each day taking up more and more space in my womb, more and more space in me. It was living off my flesh, feeding on my energy. It seemed so monstrous, this metamorphosis, the foetus and I entwined as one. My body that once contained only fear was now shielding this new life. A body that was and wasn't mine, a body hard to recognize and impossible to control. My life trickled through the umbilical cord that connected us and flowed into the baby.

STOP THREE

Four Colours Cross

BLUE

Will I ever start loving her? Will I be a good mother?
    In the silence I sense fear sidling in, bubbling under my skin.
    In the silence my thoughts spill down like ink.
    They are dark blue.

§

The lump on my thigh had begun to settle, but the pain seemed
to get stronger. I had bumped my leg against the metal frame of
the bed; it hurt for a moment, then stopped. But the mark formed,
a round shape, dark blue in the middle, overflowing to indigo in
the periphery. I didn't dare cross my legs; I sat upright at work
and pressed my knees together. I'd always been like that, since
I was a child. From a young age, even the slightest pressure on
my body caused my skin to discolour, and even placing ice cubes
on it wouldn't help.

    I imagined how people could see my pain through the skin.
Like a firefly in the dark, I was sending signals, making its existence visible, shouting silently for help.

I was lying in the crack of time between his fist poised an inch away from my face and the throbbing pain that I knew would follow; a moment in which the bone of my nose would crack then everything in front of my eyes would dissolve into light; a white spot

the speck of dust in the air froze in time, as if afraid to land on me and multiply the agony to infinity; the fear paralysed me; I stopped breathing, waiting for all the horrible things to follow

the words transformed into whispers, spilling down from the edge of the evening and turning into icicles

then he poured another glass of rum, dropped a couple of ice cubes into it, went out on to the balcony and sat on the bench he had made himself a few days before, his foot shaking nervously; at the same time, my mother was placing ice on my face to numb the pain, her sadness flowing from her eyes and subsiding in me; I was absorbing it while she was mopping my wounds with a cotton wool ball

– hold on a little longer

she said

how much longer, mum?

I never asked her this

RED

I thought I could escape, hide under the table, under the bed, in the wardrobe, lock myself in the bathroom, but he would always come and find me. How was he able to see me then, when he didn't notice me the rest of the time, as if I were invisible to him, as if I was nothing, the non-existent daughter?

he would find me and grab me by the neck; I wished my fear would make my body numb, but instead it multiplied the pain a thousand times; hunched up on the floor, I felt his hand cutting through my skin and into my stomach, taking everything from there and leaving a void, scooping my guts out with his fingers the same way he used to scoop the pumpkin seeds out with that same hand

the wet sensation on my lips would give way to the metallic taste flowing down my throat; my cheekbones would burn, their redness turning into blue like the blueness of dusk

it's ok, I thought, it's good that it hurts; it means I am still alive

– How are you feeling today?
  – Fearful.
  – What does your fear look like?
  – My fear is a stray dog, starving with hunger. It's feeding on my flesh; each day I throw him a little bit of myself so that he does not come in the night and swallow me whole.

in the neighbourhood where we lived, there were many stray dogs; each evening they gathered in packs around the bins in front of the block of flats; some of them barked deeply, hoarsely; others groaned and growled, like the wheezing of a dying old man; their fur was shabby, their teeth chattering, their eyes flashing in the darkness

– along with their stench, they spread infections too, so stay away from them my mum used to warn me

once, a neighbour decided to feed them; she carried them a bag of bones and dry bread; instead of eating the food, the dogs swooped all over her

– these are the times we live in; we are all starving, even the dogs

some other neighbours whispered; they also spread the rumour that her wounds were so deep you could see her bones

walking with my father, we neared the dogs; they watched us fiercely, but didn't approach us

– dogs don't like the meat of a drunken man

grandma said when I told her about it later

WHITE

On the train to work, I came across an article about the benefits of breastfeeding. Not only is mother's milk best for the baby, as it contains all the nutrients necessary for her to thrive, the text said, but it also helps to build an emotional bond between mother and child. The expression 'nursing mother' caught my eye and made me feel somewhat ugly, as if my sole purpose was to provide milk for the baby when it's born. All I was able to think about was seeing myself like a cow. In addition, the article continued, it is easy and convenient.

I get it. You don't need to boil water, wait for it to cool, count the spoonfuls of dry formula and wonder if you've put in two or three, because it's past midnight and you've lost your ability to count. Especially if you've fed your baby less than a couple of hours ago. Since then you've been holding it in your arms, rocking from side to side for what seems like an eternity, because the anti-colic drops don't help and the baby keeps screaming as if you are attempting to kill it. And perhaps you do want to kill it or lock it in the other room then sleep for a few hours straight. But no, you are a mother and mothers don't do that, mothers have all the strength and patience in the world, that's what people say. I didn't know at the time...

But these things were not written in the article; it was all about the benefits of breastfeeding.

– I will give you a bottle of breast milk from a nursing pig; put three drops of it in his meals, three times a day; but be very cautious, sweetheart; be careful your father doesn't catch you while doing it, see you dropping three drops onto his plate, because it will go from bad to worse and he won't stop drinking, and we won't stop him from beating you and your mother

that's what my grandma used to say, whispering, arched over my head, but she never gave me that bottle of breast milk; she was afraid that my father would catch me, and it would go from bad to worse

INVISIBLE

The nights are long. The pills don't help. The old feeling returns, tracing my steps into adulthood.

I shatter and scatter into a million pieces each night, when the old fear pins me to the wall, when the fear is an angry stray dog.

I remain dispersed on the floor all night; then in the morning I reassemble myself again, glue up the slits of my existence, wash my face and open the door to welcome the new day.

staring at the toilet, six years old and barefoot, the horror struck me

— mum!

— what's wrong, baby?

— there are worms in my poo!

— let me see... yeah, calm down, these are just intestinal worms; I'll take you to the doctor tomorrow

— just intestinal worms? but what are they?

— well... little worms, you see

— how did they get in my poo?

— you've probably eaten something unclean; I've told you how important it is to wash the fruit well

— well, maybe I forgot to wash the apple at school once; but it was a long time ago

— maybe the worms have been in your intestines since then

— they were in my tummy without me knowing? and for such a long time? how is this possible? it's the first time I've noticed them today!

— just because you haven't noticed them until now, it doesn't mean that they weren't there all the time

People say that such things don't happen these days.

Mum wanted us to keep it a secret, what was going on at home every night. We didn't want people to talk about us behind our backs, so we kept mum.

I thought that if I remained quiet for long enough, if I pretended that none of it was real, perhaps it would stop happening. And with it, my unhappiness would disappear.

When I didn't see the worms, they didn't exist.

STOP FOUR
Viewpoint Bridge

– Why did you miss our session last week?
   – Sorry, it was my birthday.
– Oh, was it? Happy birthday then. Did you do anything special?
   – No. I don't celebrate my birthdays.
– Why not?

the bike was a birthday present from my grandparents; my dad and I went to the park so he could teach me how to ride it; I fell when he stopped holding the bike without telling me; I hurt my knee, cried, and he screamed at me that I could not learn; in the end I decided I didn't want that bike and my parents sold it; mum cleansed the wounded knee with antiseptic and covered it with a plaster

a few years later, while I was playing with the kids on the streets of our neighbourhood, one of them came with her brand new bicycle with a shiny indigo metal frame and everyone was asking to borrow it for a quick circle around the block; I was afraid I would fall again, but I was more afraid of the others laughing at me because I couldn't ride a bike, so I also joined the line; when my turn came, I got up and, after a few wobbles, I was already riding it like a pro; I was so happy and proud of myself

I ran home and declared my new skill before even taking my shoes off; I was brimming with excitement

my father found an old bike somewhere and over the weekend, he repaired it, changed the tyres, and gave it to me to ride it on the street

in my family, dad always used to mend things like appliances when they didn't work; mum used to fix things between us which my dad had broken

On the way back from nursery, Ka starts explaining to me vigorously how she fell in the playground while riding a bike and hurt her knee. She gets into the role: tears, crying, as if she had fallen a moment ago. People on the street turn towards us; the parents with understanding, the rest mostly with annoyance. I stop and squat in front of her, taking her arms firmly.

– Ka, it's OK, stop crying, please. I'm sure it's not that painful. You're a big girl, right? Please stop this now, will you?

The crying intensifies and her face turns red; she crouches down on the pavement and I feel the sweat trickling down my back. The scene is turning into a tantrum and I feel helpless, a failing mother.

– Ka, sweetheart, what do you want me to do?

– Mummy's kiss makes the pain go away, she says, and points towards the knee. The skin on her knee is hardly grazed, but I waste no time and kiss her gently, give her a cuddle and promise to put a nice pink princess plaster on it when we get home. She stops crying immediately, her face lights up, she takes my hand and shifts her story to something else, about a game she played with her friends.

She won't stop talking.

I won't stop listening.

one winter, while playing with the other kids at nursery, I broke a window by accident; I don't recall how but I do remember the teacher coming to me, frowning and saying that the window was shattered beyond repair, and that my father must now pay for it; I felt so scared of what my father would do to me when he found out; something else would also be beyond repair

As a little girl, I often refused to eat for days. Doctors examined me, X-rayed my stomach, made me pee in plastic cups, but none of them could find a reason for my digestive problems. I was becoming underweight and puny, and the more my parents forced me to eat, the more insistently I refused.

My mother swore that she'd never seen such a fussy eater as me. She would cook two different dishes per meal, so if I didn't want to eat one, I could at least try the other. Finally, after hours spent at the table, doing everything possible to make me swallow just one bite, she would throw everything in the toilet. The toilet was not like me; it devoured everything. I felt terribly guilty that I could not eat these few bites to make my mum happy. But even the thought of soup would make me feel sick; its smell, like a big intestinal worm, going through my nostrils, finding its way into my stomach, irritating my guts, made me feel nauseous.

when mum went to the hospital to give birth to my sister, I didn't let anything get into my mouth, despite my dad's forceful efforts

I vividly remember three things: her brief kiss on my forehead just before slipping into the ward; the nightgown that the midwife gave her, which was coated in stains that no bleach had been able to remove; and the smell of soup coming out of the ward when she opened the door to the corridor leading to the birth centre

was that smell really there or did I imagine it? I am not sure now; I can no longer trust my memories

when my mother was admitted to the birthing ward, dad poured the cognac from the bottle down the sink and made a promise never to drink again

back at home on the third day when mum and the baby were discharged, we all sat in the bedroom studying my little sister

– look

he said

– your sister is only a few days old, and already she eats more than you do

§

I watched him rolling up his sleeves, leaning over the plate to sniff the smell of the pork chop; jabbing the meat with a fork, he started cutting it with a knife; cutting it piece by piece, bringing it to his mouth, chewing loudly, swallowing it, his lips greasy and shiny, piece by piece, until finally he ate it all

piece by piece, he was cutting me, slicing me away from my flesh and my sanity, every night, chewing, swallowing, turning me into nothing, because he didn't want me to take any space in his heart, despite my being his daughter *and so, while disappearing slowly from his life, I was looking straight into his eyes, hoping he would decide to save at least a fraction of me*

Pregnancy changed my eating habits; the one good thing, I suppose. I started eating for two, as they say. Although it didn't show on me. When the midwife weighed me during my seven-month visit and said, looking worried, that I was only eight stone, I reassured her that I'd take immediate action and bought a six-inch cake from the nearby bakery. It looked like Mum's cakes, the ones she used to bake for my birthdays when I was little, three classic sponge layers with chocolate and butter icing in between, and fluffy caramel cream on top. I ate it all by myself during my lunch break at work.

– This is to celebrate, you see, I've never been eight stone in my life before, I told a colleague, who was watching my strange ritual in shock.

– When I think about it, I too would be celebrating with a cake if I ever managed to get down to eight stone, she replied, and dunked a chocolate chip biscuit into her tea.

the doctor said that there was no obvious reason for the stomach cramps, for the diarrhoea, for the vomiting; that there was simply no apparent cause of the abdominal ache

because it's invisible, I thought, but said nothing

– it's probably something temporary and it will pass

he explained

so many years I've been waiting for it to pass, I thought

– it's simply stress-related

he finally concluded

nothing is so simple, I thought

– these doctors are a complete waste of time

my father said angrily

– they always wash their hands, saying it's stress-related when they're absolutely clueless about the diagnosis; they know nothing

maybe he knew, I thought, but remained silent

I remained silent again

People stopped asking my mother what had happened when they noticed her tense face, her dishevelled hair, her shaking hands. Just by looking into her eyes, they could sense the ache in her back, in her chest, in her stomach. There was no need to ask; every bit of her was telling stories that no one wanted to hear.

*I'd been coughing for a few days and had a fever; my parents kept me
off school, but I was feeling so unwell I couldn't even bear to watch tv*

*mum decided to experiment with an old remedy, a last try before
the doctors put me on antibiotics; on the bedside table she placed a jar
of lard, a bottle of rakia and some black pepper; I took my pyjamas
off and she dug her fingers into the lard, warming it up between her
palms and rubbing it over my chest; when she touched the area around
my breasts, I screamed in pain*

— what's wrong?

*— it hurts there, around my nipples; do you think it's something
serious?*

my mother pressed the area gently with her fingers and smiled

*— it is serious indeed; your breasts are forming; you will become
a woman soon*

I didn't know that to be a woman means to hurt, mum, I didn't know

I took Milo with me back to my home country only once, a few months after we first met. It was late summer; the flights were affordable and the alcohol cheap. He loved it all: food, nature, people. My mum didn't speak English and he'd only learned a few words in Bulgarian, so a conversation between them without me in the room to translate seemed impossible. Yet I would find them in the kitchen 'talking', taking it in turns to say a sentence in their respective language, hand gestures and facial expressions to the rescue. It was funny to watch them. My mum seemed to like him. She'd rush to place dishes in front of him on the table, offering second and third helpings the moment he emptied his plate. My sister wasn't in town, but she promised to visit us in London.

Milo wouldn't stop comparing everything to how things were back in England. He mostly talked positively.

– Oh, these tomatoes taste great! And they're huge. No wonder most British people dislike tomatoes; it seems we've never tried the real thing. And the Greek yogurt, it tastes delicious!

– It's not Greek; it's Bulgarian, I corrected him. Google it and you'll see that the bacteria that turns milk into yogurt is called bacterius bulgaricus, because it was discovered by a Bulgarian doctor more than a hundred years ago.

I wasn't sure why I felt the need to defend this fact.

– Are you proud? Milo asked me.

– Why would I be? It wasn't me who discovered it.

Later, I thought of all the historical layers in our subconscious which are often triggered without us even noticing. The feeling of pride, those little tingles when a link to someone great from your tribe is detected, surface immediately. It's funny how easily we connect. It's the same with negative feelings too, like the lingering shame from historical events which happened generations ago.

I was a bit annoyed that Milo had only noticed the worn-out perceptions of my home country. I promised myself I'd buy English-language books by Bulgarian writers I liked, so he could learn about something different and more substantial than yogurt and tomatoes.

He didn't say anything about the pretty blonde girl sitting at the table next to us in the café – long legs, short skirt, fake boobs – but I noticed the way he kept looking at her. That evening we had great sex. I wasn't sure if he was making love to me or imagining that girl from the cafe.

He would also say less positive things. Like, why were all the TV ads for junk food followed by ones for over-the-counter medicines for diarrhoea or constipation? I didn't have an explanation, so I laughed instead. Also, why did people smoke in restaurants when smoking was forbidden? I couldn't explain this either, but it wasn't funny this time, so I just shrugged.

To distract him from urban trivia, I booked a villa in the heart of the Rodopi mountains, hired a car and we drove there the next day. I took him to caves, showed him around small, almost dead villages with a few old houses and a bunch of elderly people nearing a century of their lives. I told him beautiful magical stories about this place. About mystical forest girls living in the deepest shadows in the mountains, going out at night and dancing naked under the moonlight; how if a man happened to see them and take one of them for a wife, they would give him a child and leave, as they were not made for a domestic life; how they preferred and guarded their freedom. That night we had sex again and it was even better than before. The next morning, we drove back to the city.

In the evening, Milo asked me to show him my old photos. My mum gave me the albums she kept on the top shelf of the wardrobe. I cleaned off the thin layer of dust with a sleeve before I opened them, and we both sat cross-legged on the floor, studying my childhood. I was startled by these photos. They looked somehow staged, carefully hiding what was beneath this ordinary-looking family, with ordinary-looking children, suggesting the life we lived was also an ordinary one. We had only fed the camera with happy-looking moments, hiding away the perturbing ones. Milo didn't notice anything unusual. I had kept my secret from him religiously, afraid my past would make me unattractive in his eyes.

The tension between the recollection of reality and the fabricated life in these pictures was unimaginable. The evidence had been erased as though it had never existed, as if I'd made it all up. Walking down the corridors of my memory, I felt lost.

On the TV screen two women were comparing the whiteness of their clothes: a stain remover advert. I switched it off, poured myself a glass of rum from the bottle my mum kept for special occasions and tucked the albums away at the back of the wardrobe where they belonged, hidden from me and from everyone else.

STOP FIVE

Safe Space Grove

My home was not my safe space, so I kept building dens and forts under the table, and doll's houses big enough to swallow me whole, to give me an illusory sense of protection because there was nowhere else to hide. My home was not safe for any child.

Milo, and what we shaped together, were supposed to be my safe space, but instead they turned into this icky, gooey substance I created while trying hard to avoid attachment at any cost. It seems to me now that I had glued myself to the kind of life in which I'd previously sworn never to be trapped.

Did something slip away from me over the years?

Something, or maybe someone?

eeny, meeny, miny, moe
catch a tiger by the toe

I used to play hide-and-seek with the kids in the neighbourhood; they always found me, so I had to count most of the time while the rest were hiding

I stood by the fence and counted to ten and later, when I'd learned to count to twenty, I counted to twenty before opening my eyes

the children ran and hid in their secret places, so I had to go and look for them; it used to take me ages to find them and finally, once I grew tired and gave up, I'd go back to the fence and shout: here I am, I found myself

– no, that's not how you play hide-and-seek

someone would shout with irritation and all the kids would come out of their hiding places

– you have to find us, you silly, not yourself; how could one find oneself, anyway?

I would have no answer; I was curious to know that too; how could one find oneself?

eeny, meeny, miny, moe
catch...

the game suddenly changes and I realize I am alone in the room with my father; I've learned by now to count to ten, to twenty, to infinity; I close my eyes and count, floating above my body, looking from above

– you have to hide, my girl, go

I hear his voice hissing through his teeth

the game has reversed and I'm not the one chasing the others;
I don't know what to do, I don't know where to hide, I run, stumble,
he catches me, he always finds me, huddled at the bottom
   of my fear
   go away from here

— go away from here! get your friends and leave the house! now!
   his ominous roar pushed me out onto the street; my friends were
in shock from the scene they had just witnessed
   — what happened? why did he yell at you like that? he's the father
we all envy; he's the father who organizes discos on your birthdays and
entertains us all night, who coaches our basketball team and helps us
win all the games; he's the one who plays the guitar while we sing out
of tune; he makes us feel important, funny and interesting when our
fathers do not; that's why we all envy you at school, for the smiling,
funny, supportive father; we envy you secretly so we don't offend
our own fathers
   what they didn't know was that while their fathers were teaching
them to play the triola or the piano (when all they wanted was to play
outside), my father was disciplining me because he loved me; he was
hitting me with love, slapping me with love, kicking me with love
   and when I grew up, I didn't know how to love men who didn't
hurt me
   because all I knew was that pain was love and love was pain; two
words interwoven, like a knitted pullover wrapped around my existence
   — envy me
   I told them
   — he's all this, too

The story no one told me, the one I had to grow old enough to piece together.

Everyone at school secretly envied him because his father was a captain, and not any old captain, but a naval captain of the first rank. He even tried to be proud of his father himself, imagining him, tall and handsome in his pristine white uniform, sailing his ship on the ocean. The ship was surrounded by water from here to the rest of the world, sometimes calm, sometimes stormy.

There were times when he was afraid that his father would not return.

He was my father's father, absent from home and from his children's life.

Other times, he was secretly afraid that his mother would not return in the morning after being in someone else's home for the night, because she must have been dying from the unbearable loneliness without her husband. His father was probably also dying from loneliness, but being on the ship in the middle of the ocean, there was nowhere else to go.

He, being the older sibling, would heat up the dinner for himself and his sister and then tuck her up in bed with the lullaby his mother used to sing when they were both younger. Only nine, he would then sit in his bed next to his sister's, looking into the darkness, meek, feeling abandoned.

While growing up, he grew so used to being alone and unloved that he never learned how to become a father who could love.

A father who could love me.

my father's sister loved to visit us at home, especially on my birthday, when mum used to make a delicious cake with three layers, chocolate and butter filling and fluffy caramel cream glaze, and on top of this, her homemade biscuits, meringues and crème brûlée

my father's sister used to come with her husband and daughter in the afternoon for coffee and cake and stay for dinner too; mum served them soup, followed by the main and then the dessert; to help, I folded napkins, while my father was raising glasses filled with cognac, saying cheers with every sip as a spell for good health

my father's sister used to leave with her husband and daughter when the cognac in the bottle had been finished and when the quarrels started; they always left when the plates were empty and my dad's good mood was completely gone

my father's sister is not my mother's sister; sometimes I think she's not a sister of my father either

– How are you feeling?
  – Imbecilic.
  – Why is that?
  – I am too imbecilic to know.

when I was sixteen, a friend of mine lent me his camera, a russian praktika, one of those vintage roll film slr cameras that were too expensive for a non-photographer to buy; I marvelled at the magical transformation of light onto the film; soon, capturing front doors became my new passion; old wooden doors, village-house doors, modern pva doors, doors with ornaments; I dedicated the whole film to these doors

when I went to my friend's place so he could show me how to develop the film, I realized that I'd inserted it wrongly and so nothing had been captured

I stayed there leaning against the wall with my hands covering the shame blushing over my face, devastated, and started crying; my friend tried to kiss me on the lips, to make me feel a little bit better; he defended himself when I pushed him away and stared crying louder; he gave up and left me alone in the darkroom, creasing the wasted film in my fist

why was I so sad over a film? or was it the missed chance of an exit from reality that I was mourning?

In the night, when I was still and quiet, the baby would start moving, stretching, pushing the womb walls, kicking, just like the bird that flew into my grandma's house when I was little, desperately trying to find the way out. I would instinctively place my hands over the bump, calming the baby down.

– It's OK, my little bird. I'm here. Please, be patient; hold on a little longer.

Then I'd imagine I heard their voice:

How much longer, Mama?

STOP SIX
Homestead Hill

In pregnancy, cells from the foetus are smuggled through the placenta into the mother, binding with hers and remaining there forever. I used to picture how my baby would be born soon, knowing that they would leave a permanent trace in me, a cellular contrail. The thought was both fascinating and intrusive. Where does my body end and the baby's one begin? What's theirs and what's mine to keep?

Sitting on the yoga mat, straight back, bump too big to allow me to bend forward to reach my feet, I took a deep breath in… one, two, three… and exhaled. I imagined the child in my womb. I imagined how they would be born soon and how they would become mine: my responsibility, my worries, my sleepless nights. Then, I promised myself to encode only love in them, and no fear.

the summer was hot and muggy; the days were long and stretched into nothingness; the beach was covered in bodies, many naked bodies, male and female, suntanned flesh; some women wore half bikinis, their breasts freely available to the male gaze; big, small, young and round, others had given in to the law of gravity

I am sitting on the beach towel next to my dad; my mum and sister are building a sandcastle a few steps away; I'm twelve and my own breasts have started to form, and with them, my sense of shyness has erupted; I attempt to put on my bikini top when my father stops me

– what are you doing

he asks

– you're still a child, you don't need a top

– but people are watching me, dad; I'm ashamed

– there's nothing to be ashamed of; you will start wearing a top when I say so; it's not for you to decide

he says, and I hug my knees to hide my nakedness and desperation

I didn't have anything of my own, not even my own room, and never complained

but that day he took away my own body, possessed it as though it was his right to do whatever he demanded, depriving me of my choice

The invitation to join a friend's garden party came last-minute but Milo and I had no plans for the evening, so we bought a bottle of Prosecco and a few beers and went along. The irony of being invited to all those meat-heavy barbecues when both Milo and I were vegetarians. Somehow this always became a topic for carnivorous conversations. As people chewed pork chops and licked oily fingers, their mouths spat jokes at our expense. It didn't even occur to them that being a vegetarian was a matter of personal choice, as personal as the choice to decide to wear a blue T-shirt instead of a green one, for example. Public opinion is an interesting animal. By inertia, people are expected to follow the socially approved norms until the minority becomes a majority, but that takes a long time to come about, a lot of barbecues and a lot of conversations to happen without running out of patience.

Going to bed later that night, I couldn't sleep and stayed awake for hours. From an ostensibly innocuous chat about my preference for a plant-based diet, my thoughts sank much deeper, into an inner discourse about choice. I drew parallels with the expectation placed on women to reproduce, as though this was not a matter of personal choice. Was society right to impose such a role on all women? Being someone on my way to becoming a mother, had I confined myself within the same expectation, had I been ambushed in the same reproduction narrative? A matryoshka, pregnant with another one, who will one day become pregnant with another one, and so on.

On the train in the morning, I shared my thoughts with Milo. His reply surprised me.

– Well, obviously! The female body is created to reproduce itself, to give birth to children and to continue the generations.

Otherwise, it's like having a fast, expensive car and keeping it in the garage without ever driving it.

He seemed pleased with this comparison. I felt trapped on the train, which was packed as usual, people keeping their heads down, looking for their little escapes on social media and liking the lives of others. A faint recollection of a past event brought a sense of déjà vu; my body was and was not mine. Luckily, the train reached my stop; I wished Milo a nice day and rushed to get off.

my mother was crying in the other room; I could hear her hushed sobs; I wanted to approach her, hug her, clean her wounds, put a plaster on her sadness, but we stood there in silence, I on one side of the wall, she on the other, both nestled in our feeling of power-lessness

dad left for work in the morning and closed the door behind him; I took a deep breath, something I used to do every time he left home, when it was finally just me, my sister and my mum; it was the gulp of air we all needed to survive

I opened the door and found her still in bed; most other mornings she would already be in the kitchen preparing breakfast, wrapped in her gown with the yellow flowery pattern, smiling, her eyes sinking into the deep blue circles underneath them; but not that morning

– don't be afraid

I heard her saying while attempting to roll towards me

her face was not hers; it looked perturbed, crumpled; she leaned on her elbows and attempted to get up, but convulsed in pain and collapsed on the pillow

I wanted to hold her, but I was afraid I would hurt her more; I didn't move; I stopped breathing; we looked at each other and cried

– I will stay home today to fix myself

she said

make-up wouldn't do; nothing could cover the traces of last night, of his punches and kicks, of his violence branded all over her body

after school I ran home like mad; mum was still lying in bed; I sat down next to her

– everything will be fine, mum, I'm here now, don't worry

she crouched down and placed her head over my knees; I started stroking her hair gently; feelings of rage, sadness and panic were overwhelming me; I fainted for a brief moment from the sudden inflow of adrenaline; I imagined myself going after my father and crushing his face but I knew I had to stay; I knew I had to play the adult now, not realizing how dangerously the roles of mother and daughter were reversing

– close your eyes, mum; don't cry, please; everything will be all right

we both started planning how, as soon as she recovered, we would leave that place, how we would escape together, and I'd care for her as if she were my child, and how I would keep her away from harm

– tomorrow I will go to the doctor for a medical certificate, for the court

she said, and I trusted her, I believed she would do it for real this time, that she would take that first step and leave him, that she would give herself a chance to live

(she did go to the doctor, who examined her, x-rayed her and prepared the medical certificate, stamped and signed, as it should be; she slipped it temporarily into the top drawer, under the pile of bills, so my father wouldn't find it; years later it was still there, stranded in between the old bills)

then I did my homework; my dad came back from work and I took my sister to the other room to give mum and dad space to talk; sometime later, mum called for dinner

– I don't want to have dinner with him

I said

– stop this nonsense now; he promised he would change

mum replied

– how could you believe it, mum? I will never forgive him!

she shut me down

– what is there for you to forgive?

My mother's only ally was my father, the man who abused her daily. That family, that home, that life; it was all a promise she'd made to herself. It was a dream that my mother was desperately trying to reach and fulfil, and so she was prepared to give him a million second chances, to close her eyes to the obvious, to pretend that everything was fine. It wasn't easy but she kept going, kept tolerating, kept dreaming.

This I realized years later, while thinking about my own life.

§

– How are you feeling today?

  – Hateful.

  – What do you hate most?

  – Films with happy endings, red cloves, and the sound of men peeing on the street.

  – Just that?

I hated watching him dancing with my mother on new year's eve, buying her red cloves on her birthday or on international women's day (before pouring some cognac), holding her hand when walking down the street, kissing her lips, her neck, her hands, or the way he used to pinch her behind when she wore a skirt

I felt sorry for her, for having to endure all this; I pitied her for having to fake a smile for him, to talk to him kindly and gently, to agree with him, to pretend to love him

but I hadn't realized that it was my job to hate him for both of us, because she never pretended

she loved him for real

A French guy I met on a Friday night in those early years in London, whose name I can't recall, said during a long and enjoyable chat over many glasses of wine, first at the pub where he bought me the first drink and then at his place where we continued drinking well into the early hours, that you have two choices. To accept that everything in the world is connected, or that it is not. Although my life was already broken at that point, I chose to believe that things and people were interlinked. That there was a reason for everything, and that one day I'd discover it.

§

Ka is making a fuss this morning about taking her doll to the nursery. She cries and says the doll will miss her during the day, insists that we take her with us, hold her hand like a real child. It's one of those baby dolls my mum bought for Christmas, one that closes its eyes, makes sucking sounds when you put the dummy into its mouth, cries when left untouched for too long.

– This is just a doll, Ka. It's not a real baby.

– It is real, Mum. I speak to her when you're busy on your laptop. I tell her secrets. She listens. She knows everything about me.

– What secrets, Ka?

I jumped for joy when my father started making a list of the gifts we wanted him to bring from czechoslovakia

– I want a doll, but one of those with a beautiful layered dress and eyes that look real; and at least three packs of colouring pencils

I said, giving him my order

it was the end of december; he was going there for a few days on business, and these gifts would nicely find their place under the christmas tree; I couldn't wait

but just as my father left, I was diagnosed with hepatitis and was admitted to hospital; just my luck; not only could I not open my presents on christmas day but I also had to spend the whole christmas holidays in a hospital room with five other pale kids like me

every morning and evening we peed in small, labelled plastic bottles and placed them on the shelf next to our beds; we queued for a portion of stew, from which we ate no more than three spoonfuls; as this was the infectious ward, no visits were allowed

we, the children with hepatitis, were in the ward on the second floor, and the meningitis patients were on the third one, just above us; the doctors left in the evening and only a few nurses stayed overnight; the girls laughed, chased by the boys from the ward on the other side of the corridor, while the rooms above us remained silent

a couple of days before christmas, it started snowing; through the frosted windows we watched it falling and covering the frozen ground; by the evening, everything was white

after the last doctor's visit for the day, the usual bustle started; the boys came and began to chase us, filling the pillowcases with snow that they'd managed to scoop up from the windowsills and bombarding us with snowballs; we screamed and laughed, and we all enjoyed it hugely *a loud bang; a snowball blasted the window from outside and left snow marks on the glass; could this be the boys, we wondered; they can't be so crazy as to escape the guards and go out, I thought; we all rushed to see what was going on; in the street, just below our room, my father stood, grinning, with a snowball in his hand*

– who is this man?

the children looked puzzled

– my father

I muttered

– open the window!

he shouted

before I could open my mouth to say no, one of the children had done it

at that moment, dad threw the ball straight into the room

– now it's your turn, girls, come on! scoop some snow from the windowsill and see who hits me first

he said while turning his back to get ready for the coming snowballs, still laughing loudly

the children didn't need a second invitation; they started picking up the snow with freezing hands, making balls and throwing them at my father; he was giggling, leaping back and forth like a forest dwarf, and the kids around me were screaming with joy; when there was no snow left on all the windowsills in the ward, he waved me goodbye and blew me a kiss

– what about the presents from czechoslovakia?

I shouted after him

– they're waiting for you under the christmas tree

he replied, staggering to the left and to the right then melting into the darkness

– you have such a great father; I wish mine was like him

my neighbour in the next bed whispered before going to sleep later that night; I looked at her, didn't say anything and just nodded slightly

—

after the christmas holidays, the doll from czechoslovakia occupied the shelf above the tv; it remained there for years quietly watching our lives, like a naughty guest who had outstayed its welcome, and collected our family secrets under its layered dress; with its white porcelain face and black ringlets, it stood silently with a frozen smile and kept everything to itself

– we are a family and we must have no secrets from one another

my father once said when I took a gemstone bracelet from mum's jewellery box and lost it at school that same day

What I didn't know back then was that my father wasn't going abroad on business but to be with another woman. Didn't I see my mother's eyes every time that trip was mentioned? Didn't I feel her sadness, her jealousy, her humiliation?

The Czech doll looked just like that woman; with dark, curly hair and a white waxy face. Would I have still wanted that doll, if I had known? With my pencils he wanted to paint a new life with a new woman and one day new children, perhaps; would I still want those pencils?

When my father arrived in Prague, it turned out that the address his mistress had given him when they met on the beach during the summer did not exist. My father tried to call but she wouldn't answer the phone. Feeling tricked and having no money to waste on hotels and nothing else to do, he bought the doll, pencils and a return ticket, and caught the train home.

I wished I knew what he had told my mother, standing by the door when he returned.

§

In those first months while we were dating, Milo and I loved going to parties and dancing. He was an exquisite dancer. He didn't need a dance floor; just a few beats would be enough for him to grab my hand, press my body against his and twirl me to the rhythm. I could see how the other women were looking at him, thinking perhaps they could do better than me, imagining themselves in his arms, their bodies pressed against his.

He was angry at me every time I dared to dance with another guy. He would get jealous, furious, question my moves, their reasons for inviting me, the placing of their hands on my hips.

At first I tried to explain it was just a dance, but he didn't want to hear. He wanted me for himself; no one else was allowed to get any part of me.

With time, I somehow accepted it – or decided to let it go to avoid confrontation – and stopped dancing completely.

Slowly, other rules took shape along the continuum of things I had to let go of, and they sucked away my freedom like a vacuum cleaner. No evenings out with friends unless he joined me, no sports classes, no drinks after work. He loved me and wanted to keep me for himself. That's what he said, and at first I believed him.

At the Christmas party he didn't see me watching him, but I was there, invisible to him. I noticed how, when the band started playing a slow song, he didn't look for me but instead grabbed the hand of the dark-haired woman in a black satin dress who he'd been chatting to all night, pressed her tightly to his body, his fingers moving slowly down her naked back towards her hips. She took off his glasses and placed them on a nearby table, then slid her fingers through his hair. The intimacy of this gesture struck me like a slap, but I remained shadowed in the corner, pretending not to have noticed, mute.

I was there and I wasn't. He reminded me of someone I was trying hard to forget.

§

– How did you interpret his jealousy?
– As an act of love; the love I was craving so badly.
– What did he do?
– He made me a hostage of my own appetite.

§

In today's newspaper I come across a feature about a woman whose husband killed her out of jealousy. He stabbed her between the

128

ribs with a kitchen knife, the article says. In their own house, a few metres from the room where their son slept. The woman's brother received a text from her at midnight: 'He's drunk again. I'm afraid this time he will kill me.' The brother did not see the message until the morning.

Reading the news, the memory of those Saturday mornings emerges in my head. While my mother was cooking vegetable soup for lunch, my father would sit in his armchair, his head tucked into the weekend newspaper, sipping cognac from a tall glass. He was going through the news quickly, leafing through the pages impatiently until he got to the sports section. A seamlessly ordinary Saturday that predicted another rough evening.

The knives at home were so blunt that Mum was barely able to cut the potatoes.

once, in the mountains, I was stung by a bee; my mother rubbed the place with a halved garlic clove

another time, I slammed my finger in the door; my mum ran outside and found a leaf called bear's paw in the garden, and wrapped my finger in it

when I was seven or eight, I got measles; my mother used cotton wool soaked in boiled water and a few drops of tea tree oil to soothe the itch

mum always had a cure for everything, but she knew no cure for her own suffering

Carla, a friend of mine from uni with little tits and a great interest in women's rights, announced to the group of our friends who'd gathered at the cafe after lectures that she'd decided not to have kids, regardless of the wishes of whoever she ended up marrying. She was certain about it. She had told me a story once before that I remembered.

When she was a baby, her mother took her for a walk in the park. She was young, tired and still trying to adjust to her life as a new mother. She met some friends, sat at a cafe, chatted, laughed. Then she left the cafe and walked home.

A few minutes later, Carla's mother stopped.

– My baby!

In panic, she rushed back running and found the baby sleeping in the pram, next to the table where she had left it a moment ago. Just a few minutes. But how could a mother forget?

– My mother mentioned this story only once, my friend said. As if she wanted to apologize for leaving her there, forgetting about her even for a brief moment. She wanted to confess her guilt, so she could pass the burden she had carried over the years.

My friend didn't blame her. But she also never forgot about it.

I wanted to forget, to erase events, to erase myself

how many pills are there in a pack of diazepam, I wonder; I take five; vodka; I go out

it's sunny and bright outside, too bright; I walk under the poplars, go to the park, buy a beer from the corner shop and the guy doesn't even ask me how old I am, then I drink from the bottle

I sit on the grass, soft, green grass; I see someone walking towards me, approaching me already

– hi, who are you? do you want a beer?

I ask, but I can't understand his answer

I search for the diazepam in my pocket, take five more pills; the sun shines, it blinds me, it dazzles me and I can't see anything; I get up, walk, climb stairs; where did these stairs come from? a swing; I sit on it and forget everything, there is no past, no present, time is limitless; is it time for more? I take a few more, don't know how many, a few, I lumber down the stairs, where did these stairs come from? a couple is sitting on the bench; they're talking or kissing each other, I can't see well in the glaring sun, the grass is so green, the day is so beautiful; life is so beautiful

I take the bus, centuries pass by before I get off; I feel an urgent need to run, where am I? it's my grandparents' village, it seems; I run around all afternoon, I am out of breath and out of money; I stop in front of the house and go inside; my grandparents are happy to see me but they cannot understand why I keep chasing the hens in the yard; it's getting dark, the tiredness makes my eyelids heavy; I go to bed and fall asleep at that very moment

– wake up! please wake up!

I open one eye, then the other; my mother is sitting on the corner of the bed, holding a glass of milk

– drink it, please; how are you feeling?
– I don't feel anything
I answer, then I drink the milk
she doesn't say anything
(not that she was worried sick about me all night; that she called all
my friends but none of them knew where I was; that she walked the
streets like a sleepwalker, her tears flowing, her make-up running all
over her face; that she called my grandma first thing in the morning
and my grandma told her that I was there, sleeping in the other room;
that my mum took the bus and, when she arrived, thanked god that
everything had turned out ok in the end; that she found the empty
diazepam pack in my pocket and realized that nothing was ok

that then she poured some fresh milk in a glass, her hand trembling,
and attempted to wake me up, hiding her anxiety from my grandma,
not to worry her; that she promised herself not to ask any questions;
that she promised herself finally to find the answers)

I drink the milk; its whiteness is healing, it cleanses the toxins
my mother lies down in my bed next to me, hugs me; I hug her too
and she closes her eyes, inhaling the softness of the new day

The day I received my exam results confirming I'd been admitted to study marketing in Sofia and grasped that I'd be leaving our family home for good in a couple of months, I broke down in tears. Those were happy tears, of relief. I had been waiting for that moment for so long. Like most of my friends, I felt liberated and independent.

I glanced around me, still holding the letter in my shaking hands, and memories pushed me against the wall. It was in this living room that I had collapsed on the floor when my dad had slapped me because I refused to go to the shop at midnight to buy him a bottle of cognac. It was in this kitchen that my mother had hidden the morning after he bruised her face. It was in this bathroom that my father had cut my hair short with the blunt scissors because he became frustrated every morning waiting for me to brush and plait my hair.

I had thought I would leave this home, and that, in doing so, all those memories would dissolve into nothingness. That I would start afresh in a new place and never look back. How wrong I was!

§

Those years were an in-between time, after leaving home and before being able to distance myself from the haunting past. They were also a time of preparation, studying and working part-time in a restaurant kitchen, gaining knowledge and saving money for my next step. I opened the door to my new life and jumped.

§

He was at a party, French-kissing a tall blonde girl in a short skirt, when I first saw him. I noticed his strong broad arms and tight arse, his dark curly hair stroking her pretty face. I knew the girl from uni, the *I-want-it-all-and-want-it-now* kind of girl, the only child of a corrupt politician and his housewife spouse, the nineteen-year-old doll who had a flat of her own, who came to the halls for the parties but who'd speak of our living there with disgust. The kind of girl who treats people as disposable gloves she can use once and then get rid of. The boys she used for money and gifts, the girls to help her with exams. They were a group of five girls, all daughters of rich parents, the privileged ones, who'd always hang out together and would leave a long trail of expensive perfume behind them in the corridors.

I waited patiently for her to go to the bathroom with her girlfriends while I was drinking vodka straight from the bottle, then neared him.

– You know what people say, men's most sensual body parts are the ears, I whispered, allowing my lips to touch the top of his right earlobe.

He turned towards me in surprise, briefly examining my face and body.

– Is that true?

His voice was deep and silky. He took the vodka from my hand and had a deep gulp without taking his eyes off my body.

– I don't know. You tell me.

The next thing I remember was us kissing in the darkness, his hands scooping and squeezing my buttocks. It didn't take long before Blondie interrupted, pulled me away in anger and started shouting in my face. I laughed back as though I didn't give a damn, and left, blowing him a kiss just before my swift exit. She was furious but he was already hooked on the idea of finishing what we'd started. I had slipped my address in his pocket, so a couple of hours later he knocked on the door.

I could imagine how he'd been trying to calm her down, explaining that I was some crazy bitch and he had been too slow to react and push me away, her crying, him walking her home, having a quick fuck to dissolve any suspicion so that they would remain allies, bonded by their mutual interest in money/power.

He came in, his expensive scent mingling with sweat and pheromones, pushed me towards the kitchen and, while I was undoing his jeans, took off my underwear in a swift move, perhaps well-practised, then fucked me right there over the worktop without fully undressing me. He was no good, I knew that, but I had no interest in a relationship with him. Life was too fast-moving, exciting and rich. I was desperate to catch up on what I used to crave as a child: the male affection my father never gave me. The boy was a one-night stand, one of many, the sort of fling whose briefness kept me untethered.

§

For a long time Milo and I had been spending our weekends in the company of estate agents. We looked at other people's homes, inhaling the smell of their memories, imagining our future there.

When we finally chose a place to call our own, we only had a couple of weeks to clean, redecorate and furnish it before the baby arrived. As my womb was changing, accommodating the baby growing inside, Milo was busy arranging the interior of what would become their home after the birth. I made sure not to forget to drink my pregnancy vitamins every morning while scrolling down Pinterest photos of the latest trends in home interior design. I followed parenting blogs and their 'how to' articles, despite being fully aware that none of this could be learned by reading.

We were both getting ready for the future, without knowing what this future would be like.

STOP SEVEN
Seed Lock

I t all started before taking the test, even before my period was late. Vivid dreams. Clear, brimming with freshness, with lurid colours, with life, as though the invisible film which used to blur them had been removed and they were all exposed now, raw, unrefined. My days were merging together, nauseous and heavy, while the dreams were replacing life, well contoured, with their own shape and taste, a fabric I could caress with my senses.

I dreamed once about eating peaches and their sweetness left a trace in my mouth in the morning. I dreamed about kissing a stranger, a deep, long kiss, pulling him towards me by his belt, undoing his jeans, turning around and feeling his breath on my neck. A feeling of guilt woke me up. His scent was all over my skin and for a moment I questioned whether he was indeed lying beside me.

I dreamed about a child, a little girl with blonde hair in ringlets and bright eyes; she didn't look like me.

– Hello, Mama! she said and smiled, then dissolved as though she was a reflection in a mirror.

Where has she gone? I woke up anxious, trying hard to unravel the strange message, and couldn't get back to sleep for hours. The baby started hiccupping and I placed my hands over the little knot forming on my bump, probably a foot or a hand, by the pressure of her stretching and turning inside me.

I didn't tell Milo about it, nor about any of the other dreams. They were mine, my fluffy little secrets, a blanket to wrap around my shoulders when it was cold and hostile outside.

on a cold winter sunday morning the smell of freshly made pancakes wakes me up; I get out of bed and go barefoot to the window; during the night snow has fallen; deep, fluffy snow, covering everything with its whiteness; this fairy-tale picture makes me jump for joy; I rush to the kitchen; the pancakes are waiting for me on the table, next to a jar of homemade blueberry jam

we all gather and I tuck into the pancakes like a ravenous puppy; one of the few things I eat without having to stay at the table for hours; mum spoon-feeds my sister with banana rice porridge and gives her only a small bite of pancake to try; she is licking her lips and opens her mouth again and again like a little bird; she seems to like it a lot and points her little finger towards the jam; we laugh, then I finish my breakfast and, while I am brushing my hair, my father has already prepared the sleigh; by the sea the snow rarely settles for long, so we have to hurry

mum stays at home with my sister, as it's too chilly for a little baby, and also to prepare the lunch for when we come back

I'm dressed in layers of warm clothes and wait impatiently in the corridor; there is a small window left for my eyes in between the hat and the thick white scarf covering my nose so I can barely see; we leave the house

dad holds my hand while pulling the sleigh with the other; once outside, I lower the scarf and the winter cold snaps at my face so I pull it back on; against the background of my cerise mittens, the falling snowdrops reveal their magically perfect hexagons before melting away; the streets are crammed with shiny, joyous children and I can barely contain my excitement

we walk through the subway and into the park on the other side of the street; it's already packed with kids; the sound of snow champing under our shoes dissolves into the children's hubbub the hill is over there; most of the kids are slithering on plastic bags; looking around, I might be the only one with a proper wooden sleigh; we climb up the slope; it's steep and icy; the kids look much older than me

– dad

I pull his hand

– I don't want to slide any more; it looks scary

the scarf has loosened and my nose is shining, the colour of my mittens

– what do you mean you don't want to? it snows once a year and you don't want the chance? no way; hold on tight!

he doesn't wait for an answer, pushes me to get on the sleigh and pulls it down the hill holding the rope and running as quickly as he can; the slope is already well polished by the kids with their plastic bags ahead of me; the sleigh gains speed, catches up with my father and overtakes him; he lets go of the rope but keeps running after me

– da–a–d!

I close my eyes and hold tight

after a moment, I hit the pile of crusty snow at the end of the slope, turn over and, to my horror and the kids' shock, land with aplomb, facing the ground; I can't move, frozen with shame and pain at the same time; I feel the snow on my neck, I've lost my hat and the cold crawls up my back

my father catches up with me; he starts laughing as if giving a green light to all the humiliation that is about to pour over me, allowing everyone who has hesitated up until that moment to join in the fun, pointing their fingers; their laughter reaches me as a grotesque amalgam of sounds and mooing; my dad helps me get up, shaking the snow off my coat, but I wish I could bury myself under the snow and stay there forever

I still can't shake the shame

A confession:

I've always been very bad at caring for plants. In those flats I rented over the years, I would buy many potted plants, making promises to myself to get better and take proper care of them. At first, I would water them regularly, then sometimes when I happened to remember, although most often I didn't remember at all. The plants would make an attempt to survive, then one by one the leaves would go yellow and die.

Since having a daughter, I've often had a dream about forgetting to feed her for days. I wake in the middle of the night in horror and rush to the bedroom to check on her.

the summer came and, along with it, two sisters arrived; they were from sofia, staying with their grandmother for the holidays; they were slim, long-haired and vegetarian

one afternoon, as we were sitting on the kerb in our neighbourhood, chatting and nibbling corn on the cob, the boy from the nearby block of flats, whom I had been secretly watching from a distance for several weeks, passed on his bike; I would normally look aside every time our eyes were about to meet, but this time I was on a mission to face him; I stared at him with a steady look, already feeling myself blush, but he gazed instead at the vegetarian sisters who were vigorously biting the juicy corn with their big, white teeth, licking their lips, giggling

going back home, I had at least two reasons to become a vegetarian; it was a perfect excuse not to eat meat any more, and the boy next door obviously had a weak spot for vegetarians; when I declared my decision at dinner, my father laughed

– deal

he said

– I suggest we all become vegetarians; I am personally planning to focus on the fermented fruits

then he poured himself another glass of red wine

When my mum got a birthday present, she would always leave it for a few days before unpacking and using it. To mature like an old wine, she used to say. It was hard for her to get used to new items. As well as all the new things in life.

§

– How are you feeling today?
  – Cold. Unloved and untouched for what seems an eternity. It wasn't all bad with Milo. The way he wanted me, caressed me, kissed me.
  – Do you miss him? Do you still hold on to your good moments together?

§

I would open the front door and enter the room, where I'd find him sitting on the sofa, watching the news and snacking on cheese strings, but a different kind of door remained closed in front of me which I was unable, or maybe unwilling, to open.

Even now, years later, I sometimes catch myself thinking of Milo and the things that drove us apart. I wonder about the way his mind works. He always used to be certain of things; each thing had a word, its own meaning. For him, a string of thoughts was linear and, although he said he liked to be challenged, he didn't. He is a theatre director, after all; he likes to direct. Unlike many of his acting colleagues, his views are concrete, never ambivalent. He engages with art in a way that untangles it into clear meaning, one that makes sense to him.

But life is not a play, nor is a relationship. There are no intervals between acts, no time to stop and catch your breath. I rarely spoke to him about my past. Not that I feared he wouldn't under-stand. I was afraid he'd label me like the others had. The girl of the alcoholic man on the fourteenth floor, the victim of the abuser, the survivor, which suggested there was something unspeakable preceding the act of surviving, leaving the remains behind.

I am the remains, and at the same time I am my own inception.

§

I wanted to leave him and I didn't. Who would wrap their arms around me from behind while I was cooking dinner, if I left? Who would leave 'I love you' notes next to my pillow when they got up earlier than me? Who would dance with me when the radio played our favourite songs?

I realized that, for my mother, the act of physical violence and brutality was better than not being touched at all.

In the rare quiet moments she was piling up his affection, collecting and assembling the occasional crumbs of love she would find, so that one day, when she gained the strength to leave, she'd live off these stocks of love.

She squirrelled them behind her tired skin, in the darkness under her eyes, in the premature wrinkles, making herself busy only to prolong the moment before saying goodbye.

§

I hope that Ka will understand one day, and that she will forgive me for the choices I've made. Looking back and thinking of my own mother, I didn't understand her choice to stay then. Was I selfish? Maybe. Or perhaps we all need to walk the mile, go through life ourselves, face all the obstacles and decisions we encounter on the way, so we're able to grasp it all.

§

– Mama, let's continue the story about Soraya.

– Where did we leave it last time?

– Ivan recognized her by the lake among the rest of the *samodivi*.

– Ah, yes. Listen then…

– 'It's me, Ivan, my love,' she replied when he called her name, as if casting a spell on him. She smiled, then joined her girlfriends again and kept dancing until the first sunrays.

Without realizing, Ivan had fallen asleep and didn't see where the *samodivi* had gone. But he had a plan. The next evening he returned to the exact same place by the lake, started playing his *kaval* and waited. It didn't take long before he heard the sweet melody again, and the moment the moon came up, the *samodivi* gathered by the lake and began to dance. One by one they removed their belts, unbuttoned their white shirts and left their clothes on the shore. Then, holding hands, they stepped into the lake, splashing the water, laughing. Ivan saw everything. He approached the clothes and took the ones that belonged to Soraya.

'Ivane!' He heard Soraya's voice. 'I'll do whatever you want, just don't take my clothes.'

But Ivan knew from the people's whispers that the *samodivi's* magical power was hidden in their white shirts and their rainbow belts. If a man steals them from a *samodiva*, she becomes a human woman again and obeys his wishes.

Ivan kept Soraya's clothes and locked them in a wooden chest at home, then put the key on a string and wore it around his neck day and night. Having lost her magical power, Soraya had no choice; she left the *samodivi*, married Ivan and lived with him in the village. A year later, she gave birth to a beautiful baby girl.

Soraya was fond of Ivan but was unhappy in the village, away from her friends. It wasn't her choice to marry him, and although she loved him like a brother, she was longing for freedom. Her hair lost its shine, her eyes turned grey and her laughter was forgotten by everyone, even her.

'Give me my clothes back, Ivane, a *samodiva* can't live in a village, can't keep house, can't stay with a man. A *samodiva* needs her freedom, Ivane. Please give me my white shirt and my rainbow belt,' she begged, but Ivan wouldn't listen.

He pretended not to see her sadness. He was scared that if he gave her back the clothes, she would leave him forever.

a dream

we're in a car and the car is at the top of a hill; the hill is coated in freshly cut grass; all of us are in there: my sister and I, mum and dad; it's one of those dreams in which I see myself from the side; I am in the front seat and holding the wheel, even though I'm fifteen and I cannot drive; before our eyes, the hill is steep and green

suddenly, the car starts moving downhill at full force; the next moment it starts rolling over like a scene in an action film; the car doors open (are those mannequins in the car or real people?), my father falls out of the car and continues to roll down head over heels; I watch everything without being able to influence it, I notice it from afar; we are all alive; I see how there, at the bottom of the hill, my grandparents are waving at us, waiting

I woke up tense, my hand muscles aching as if I were gripping the wheel from my dream for real

three days later, my mother packed our clothes and textbooks in three black bin bags; she also took half the books from the shelves, the china teacups that her parents gave her as a wedding present, and the photo albums; it was saturday afternoon; my father was at a football match with friends, so mum was rushing to get things packed before he got back

my sister and I were waiting in our room; being the older one, it was my job to distract my sister so we didn't get in mum's way, but instead I was sitting on the floor, trying to pacify my stomach cramps, both from excitement that it would all end soon and from fear that my father might come back and find us before we were able to escape

mum had organized everything; when the doorbell rang, she rushed to open the door; our relatives had come to take us and to offer us shelter for a day; the plan was to get the train the next morning to our grandparents and move in with them, temporarily at least

we had piled all the bags and boxes into the car when my father showed up; on any other day, he would be late, going for a few drinks after the game

but not this time

he was standing by the door, sober and confused; looking back, I wonder if he knew; had he anticipated my mother's decision? he seemed embarrassed, tried to hug mum, begged her to stay; the relatives kindly pushed me and my sister back to our room so we didn't witness the quarrel

we stood still, one ear pressed to the wall, hoping to hear what the adults were talking about; from time to time somebody raised their voice, then everyone started shouting over each other and, finally, went quiet again

hours later we were still in the room, hungry and tired, sitting in opposite corners, giving up on our impotent attempts to catch a word through the wall; it was dark, past our dinner and bedtime, but it seemed that they'd completely forgotten about us

we were about to go to bed when the door opened; my father; he walked slowly, approached my sister and hugged her

no, don't give in to him, I thought, don't listen to his apologies, his pleading voice; it's worth nothing; everything is a show; tomorrow it will be the same

the relatives stepped in after him, and, to my horror, began to bring back our luggage

what are you doing, I thought, you were supposed to be on our side! didn't you come to help us?

I raged silently but no one noticed me

I tried to catch a glimpse of my mother; she was sitting on the edge of the sofa, her face buried in her hands; she had given up again, betraying her future; she had given up, betraying me

—

after what happened that night, I lost hope; I stopped believing that one day we would leave this house and break free from the constant waves of fear and hate that were flooding my existence, suffocating me, not letting me breathe

instead, I kept on going, swallowing my rage, silently accepting the slaps on the face, the shouting through the night, his ferocious gaze, his breath smelling of cognac when he wouldn't let me go to bed without kissing him goodnight

I kept hiding my tears in the toilets at school, because no one should know that something at home was not ok, that my family was not like the others

every day I raced after school to do my homework before he got back from work, so I could take care of my sister when he started abusing my mum again, be able to call for help, he-e-elp! or run with my mother and sister to the neighbours the minute he went to the corner shop for another bottle

were there any neighbours left in the whole block of flats who hadn't given us shelter, who hadn't hidden us from him for a few hours until he fell asleep; were there any neighbours left in the whole eighteen-floor block of flats, eight flats on each floor?

each time we ran away seemed to give me a peek into a dreamed-of future, a little hope that we would soon arrive at a safe place and better times would follow

we would leave but keep the door open, slippers on, no extra pair of clothes

we would leave but never arrive, not then; we would return later that night and everything would go back in its place

– How are you feeling today?
  – Seeking.
  – What are you looking for?
  – Myself. My lost self.

§

A note in my notebook:

'Leaving one place, part of it travels with us. Passing through life, we become collectors of the feelings we've experienced in all those places we have been to. The energies mix together in a wonderful blend of light, aroma, joy and melancholy, of time and space, and cling to our minds, to our own perception of ourselves. Thus, every moment of the present is both a moment of the past and the future, from here and there.'

I tear out the page and throw it in the bin.

I don't want my past to define me like the contents page at the front of a book that sums up the narrative, organizing life into chapters.

§

I live here, in this foreign country, and there, in my childhood, as in two parallel realities. I often confuse space and time; they blend into one another. I don't know if, were I to return to the city where my life began, these parallel lines would tilt and eventually connect, create a spiral, or merge and become a whole so that I could also feel whole.

The fear is still present. It still doesn't allow me to look back without my whole being going into spasm. I remain still, weightless, at the edge of my existence.

I stretch my soul like chewing gum from that first city which marked the beginning, to all the final points I've reached in my adult life.

she leans against the door, wrapped in the gown she's worn for years, its colours fading; her hands are crossed in front of her chest because she doesn't know where else to place them; her eyes are tired, with dark circles around them, and I know she hasn't slept all night

she goes to the kitchen, makes coffee and pours it into two cups: a large one for me, a small one for her; I stopped drinking my coffee in a big cup years ago; she knows me from the days when my heart was beating deep inside her womb, and yet there are so many things about me that she doesn't know

she slices two pieces of a cake that she baked early in the morning; she places them on a plate on the table in front of me; two flies land next to them and start rubbing their feet

she chides me for not eating over the plate, crumbs falling on the ground, and I begin to admonish her about how bad the sugar she puts in her coffee is for her health, two full teaspoons

– it always tastes bitter to me

she says, then rolls her eyes and pauses

she waters the plants, so she doesn't stay still; she urges me to go because the expectation of our parting is harder than the parting itself; I stuff a piece of cake into my mouth and she gives me a few more slices wrapped in foil for the trip; I snap at her that I have no place for it in my luggage

we sip our coffee in silence and the unspoken words weigh on our tongues; I get up and move towards the suitcase, leaning against the wall in the corridor; a tear, like a raindrop, grows in the corner of her eye but stays there, still unripe; she hugs me, so I won't notice; I close the door behind me; she stays there on the other side, her head pressed towards the door, giving my echoing footsteps a send-off

I call her as soon as I arrive; only then do I tell her I love her; as I unpack my luggage, I find the cake wrapped in foil; I dig in, being careful not to let crumbs fall on the floor

so many years have passed and I still taste the bitterness of that coffee

I wanted to run away from my childhood. For years I had been thinking about this escape. I gathered my belongings and left the past out of my suitcase, careful not to take anything that would bring back memories. No photos, no items I loved, only some clothes that I would change soon anyway. I didn't want to get attached to anything or anyone. The aeroplane tore my life in half like a piece of old cloth wearing thin; everything that was familiar was left on one side, and a new life was waiting for me on the other.

It was only when I landed at the airport that I was able to inhale deeply for the first time. No one was waiting for me with a name card; there was no one there to help me with my suitcase. But there was no regret, not even nostalgia. I felt relieved, free from fear. My arrival at this strange new place brought an almost orgasmic feeling which I wasn't able to describe. It's finally over, I said to myself. I hoped that the tears on my pillow would be the only traces of my past.

Did I realize then how long these stains would remain, the scars of my past that would not heal, the scars that I, involuntarily, would drag like a scruffy teddy bear to my new relationships, new places and times, without ever being able to erase them? it always smelled of a fairy tale in my grandma's house; sometimes of those masha and the bear pirogi, another time of the cookies from carlson who lives on the roof; as soon as I got there, I started opening the kitchen cupboards and inhaled their aroma; the only thing I was told not to open was the aladdin's lamp, which was a bottle of almond aperitif, otherwise I'd free the bad spirit, grandma used to say

once, while she was cooking polenta on the balcony and the smell of fried cornflour tickled the neighbours' senses, a sparrow swung into the kitchen; it seemed scared; it skittered across the walls, around the ceiling, fluttering its wings, landing on the floor, but when I tried to catch it and put it outside, it scraped and banged against the walls; finally, it fell down and collapsed in the corner

– why did it not let me help?

I asked my grandmother, weeping

– because it's afraid

grandma replied, and hugged me

– it doesn't know that you are a good girl and probably fears things would go from bad to worse if you move nearer

it would go from bad to worse, she said, and I was beginning to understand why my mum was still there, not able for so long to leave my father and to start a new life with me somewhere else

she was like that frightened sparrow, banging her scarred body between the walls, panting, suffering quietly, nestled in the corner

no, she wouldn't have let me help her

—

grandma was constantly losing things

I would help her find them, and for a reward she always gave me some treats: cookies, waffles, you name it; sometimes she'd lose her glasses, only to find them on the bed, next to her pillow; another time she would lose her place in the queue when someone decided to push in front of her, but I would do the shopping for her

lately, she'd lost all hope

Scientists are on their way to creating a device that can read your thoughts, it says on the news today. Up to ninety-two per cent, apparently. They say it's a sensational discovery that will help people communicate freely, for example those with the syndrome Stephen Hawking had. It will also be extremely useful in police and court interrogations.

If they had invented this device years ago, Mum would have read my fears and decided to leave my father once and for all. Dad would have read her intentions to leave him, and one night he would have thrown her over the balcony, from the fourteenth floor. I would have lived with the guilt that my thoughts had killed my mum. This would have been convenient for my father, who, along with all those watching the news, would have welcomed the thought-reader helping thousands of people around the world.

Some discoveries are better placed in the future.

My mind slips to a May Day demonstration in 1986, when we all marched down the streets, waving flags, inhaling the spring air. Then we returned to our homes, ate fresh salad with our lunch, moved on with the day as if nothing had happened. Because none of us knew what had actually happened. Nobody bar the party leaders knew that a few days earlier, on 26 April, there had been an explosion at the Chernobyl nuclear power plant. A thousand kilometres away from our city, the radiation in the air was now poisoning our lungs, our bodies, our future children. The party didn't want us to know. The party wanted shiny, happy people, demonstrating and cheering those in power.

the years after the collapse of communism were hard and food was scarce, but somehow my dad's friends never stopped coming home for a drink; they used to bring bottles of all sorts of precious liquids: amber, golden, crystal clear; mum provided a salad, as well as some company

my dad's friends loved it when my father was in a good mood, when he grabbed the guitar and played the beatles; they would top up my father's cognac, empty the dishes and leave; we were left behind with empty glasses and no gaiety

– why do they make my father drink?

I asked my mother once

– they like him this way; they just don't know; it's all about perceptions

my dad's friends were not my mum's friends; nor mine

You'd be amazed to know how the news about being pregnant changed people's perceptions of me.

Family. The family felt relieved and excited. I remember the day I called my mother on Skype to break the news. It was a late Saturday afternoon; the sun had turned the walls of my bedroom warm orange and my complexion looked healthier on the laptop camera. I was four months along but had just recently accepted the definiteness of my impending pregnancy, sipping decaf coffee from my favourite ceramic mug as though holding on to the one thing that felt familiar and secure. My mum looked tired on the screen, and her hair, tied back and wrapped in a yellow fabric cloth, told me she'd been cleaning the house and tidying up all morning. Milo had just gone for a jog, so I had less than an hour to chat to her undisturbed.

– Mum, I'm having a baby. I mean, we. We're having a baby. You'll be a grandmother soon.

Despite my intention to get to the point with a clear declaration, I was mumbling already.

– What? Aw, congratulations! My baby is having a baby! How did that happen?

– Well, I won't go into details.

– Don't try to be clever with your mother. I'm so happy for you two. When are you due?

That question. A quick calculation after revealing the date led to the realization that I'd been withholding this piece of information from her for months. I noticed the excitement on her face beginning to get overshadowed by disappointment, all the questions galloping in her mind, but she remained silent and just smiled, perhaps hoping that I wouldn't have wanted to

159

worry her if something had happened to the baby in the early weeks. I felt both relieved to be sharing the news with her and guilty for not telling her the whole story. To this day, she still believes that I didn't truly mean it when I told her I didn't want to become a mother, that it was just a period, a moment of doubt as to whether I'd cope, or even selfishness, being hungry for a career, travelling, and with friends to attend to.

She never found out how scared I was at the time, keeping a baby I never planned for. There I was, hiding my unhappiness from my mother the same way she had buried hers thirty or so years ago. We were looking at each other from our sides of the laptop screen as though mirroring one another, gazing at our reflections, only separated by time. And a few deep wrinkles.

A mother and daughter tell each other everything, share their secrets, gossip and clothes, and we pretended we were like those mothers and daughters, imitating the happy lives of others, but did we even know ourselves or each other?

Then there were my colleagues. The men stopped noticing me almost immediately. No more after-work drinks invitations, no offers to make me a cup of tea, no jokes in the kitchen. Their flirty gazes gave way to sympathetic looks. I had crossed the field from being a woman to becoming a mother. While my bump was growing, I was becoming invisible. They also stopped seeing me as their competitor. I should have been glad, but I wasn't. Somehow my pregnancy decreased my authority in client meetings or creative sessions, as though cognitive impairment were a side effect of carrying a baby. The women, on the contrary, became kinder to me, perhaps also downgrading me from a potential enemy when it came to men's attention to an inflated body, growing by the day.

Then there was the parents' group, those who rushed to offer me their tips and advice and pointed out useful articles online or introduced me to their horror birth stories. The list was hefty, puffing up along with my feet.

Attachment parenting
Breastfeeding on demand
Babywearing and sling safety
Colic drops
Sleeping routines
Bath times
Baby massage
Weaning and first finger foods
Potty training
Play time and educational toys
Nursery rhymes
Baby and toddler crèches
Applying for a nursery place early on

Every mother had her own view on what was best. All of them told me I should not listen to others but should follow my instincts.

– What if I don't have any instincts just yet? I asked.

– All mothers do, they said, smiling, looking at each other in obvious agreement.

This should have been reassuring, but it wasn't. None of them mentioned anything about feeling tired, or guilty, or unsatisfied at spending their days behind closed doors with a crying baby. No one gave me advice on self-care; how to look after my body and sanity, how to stay healthy, sleep well, enjoy sex, go out with friends from time to time, and dedicate time to myself. And most surprisingly, not a single one of them mentioned the role of the father. Not a word. As though the fathers were not part of the parent–child equation, not in the early months at least. Their bodies didn't have to change, nor their minds or habits.

§

The noticeboard in the kitchen is overtaken by birthday invitations, neatly pinned, in chronological order. They are all for my daughter from the kids at nursery; around a dozen for the next couple of months, one every weekend, sometimes two or even three. She wants to go to all of them and throws a tantrum if I ask her to skip one. I want to avoid tantrums at all costs, so I make my plans around hers, confirm by email, buy presents and socialize with the parents, pretending I am pleased to hear about their current house renovation or impending holiday. Today is Erin's birthday party at the community hall across the road.

– Mama, did you know Erin doesn't have a mother, but she has two daddies?

– No, I didn't.

– Now that I don't have a dad, can I have two mums instead?

– Ka, you do have a father. He just doesn't live with us.

She puts on a disappointed face and an emerald princess dress. I plait her hair. We're running late; there is no time to do my make-up. When we arrive, the entertainer has just started and the kids have all circled her, submissive and engaged. I push my daughter gently to join them and look around for a safe corner. One of Erin's fathers offers me a cup of coffee, the other one mouths *hi* from the other side of the room. Most parents seem to know each other well and are chatting in groups. Erin's fathers are buzzing around, making everyone feel comfortable.

– Cheese and ham sandwich? they offer.

– Thanks, I'm vegan. I'm fine with my cup of coffee.

– Vegan? So you couldn't resist and joined the trend, huh?

– See, thick eyebrows à la Frida Kahlo are a trend. Mine is a choice.

The dad chuckles as if I am telling him a joke and moves on with the small talk.

I never managed fully to master the art of British small talk.

I remember how, just after I started my first job in London, a colleague spoke to me in the lift.

– How are you? she asked cheerfully, and I, feeling touched by her sudden interest in me, began to explain all about my troubles with the noisy neighbours next door, arguing all night and not letting me get any sleep.

She looked at me in surprise and with a dose of irritability, and changed the subject to the all-time-top, no-chance-to-go-wrong topic of the British weather. It was only later that I realized how naive I was, taking her question so personally, when all she wanted to hear was the short and convenient *fine, thanks.*

Nowadays, I know better. When I was pregnant with Ka, I had my answers ready for the routine questions, the same ones asked every day.

– In the fifth month.

– In August.

– We still don't know the sex, but no, it doesn't matter whether it's a boy or a girl.

– I didn't feel very well at first, but the morning sickness settled and I'm fine now.

(I spared them the details about my constant vomiting every day, sixteen weeks in a row.)

– Yes, it's my first child.

(*Why, do you think I'm too old for a first child? Being a mother is not all women's only goal in life.* I wished I could spit this in their faces, but I spared them.)

– No, I'd rather you didn't touch my bump.

I only used that last answer when someone placed their hands on my bump before even asking. In these cases, I often wanted to scream at them: *Do I touch your stomach like that? What makes you*

think it's OK for you to touch mine? How come the situation is differ-
ent because I'm carrying a baby – no, not even a baby, an embryo?

But I would remain silent and move back slightly, as persocial norms.

The woman would get overly excited.

– Ah, I think I felt it kicking.

– I doubt it, I would reply. It's most probably my stomach rumbling. I've been hungry all day.

Her hands would immediately leave my belly.

And this was how most conversations ended.

§

At first, I thought it wasn't real. I was waiting in the queue at the supermarket when I felt it. I froze. Stopped breathing for a moment, listening. I instinctively put my hand on my bump, as if to show the baby I had decoded the sign. It was light and weak, subtle. And then again, like a fluttering of butterfly wings dissolving somewhere deep inside of me, about to cause a hurricane on the other side of the world. I paid for the carrots and parsley and went out.

On the stairs in front of the store, an elderly woman, hump-backed by the years, her hands as wrinkled as her face, was selling bouquets of yellow primroses from a big bucket full of water.

– I'd love a bunch, please. I smiled and placed the note in her hand.

She looked up, as if waking from a nap. Her face seemed strange; almost all of it had been taken over by her long, wide, unusually large nose. She resembles Baba Yaga, I remember thinking, and felt ashamed of myself straight away. The woman dipped her hand in the bucket, picked out the best primrose bouquet and just before handing it to me, said:

– It smells wonderful, of new life.

I took the flowers and tucked them under my nose. They didn't smell of anything. The woman grinned with her toothless mouth, as if catching my thoughts, and nodded towards my bump. Did she mean the baby? How was she able to see the barely rounded bump under my extra-large sweater?

Then she bent even further so, looking from above, I could only see her hump, and she started digging into the rustling plastic bag on her lap. She lifted her head and grabbed my hand; in her bony fingers there was a *martenitsa*.

– Take it, girl, so you give birth to a healthy child.

I was puzzled but thanked her and left. I walked slowly, absorbing the March sun and breathing the smell of the blossoming almond trees.

For the first time since discovering I was pregnant, I looked differently at the baby in my womb. No matter whose decision it had been to conceive it, the child was still mine. They were growing and changing inside me, and I was growing and changing too; life existing in the present and the future, both my life and the baby's at the same time.

I felt the urge to buy all the flowers from that strange woman. I went back, almost running, but there was no trace of her.

a few days before the first day of march, at school, we did martenitsi in arts; we all loved the ritual of making and then swapping martenitsi as a symbol of health and new beginnings; in front of each of us, there were white and red threads, blue beads, scissors and cardboard; I began to craft my pijo and penda dolls; I twisted the threads together, winding them around the cardboard: white yarn for penda, red for pijo; I was very pleased with the result; so pleased that I didn't want to give it to anyone; my pijo and penda were tightly connected to each other with the red and white threads, like voodoo dolls; I wanted to keep them for myself

when I got home, I took a matchbox from the kitchen drawer and emptied it onto the table; with the sticks I built a house, gluing them to one another, then I lifted the walls carefully and didn't dare breathe, so it wouldn't break accidentally; when it was ready, I used the inside of the matchbox for a bed and placed pijo and penda in it; they seemed happy in this house, connected to one another; I was pleased with the result

I nested the house under the bed in my room; every day after school I took out the house with pijo and penda, played with them and shared their seeming happiness, my white magic for good luck; after a while, I forgot about pijo and penda completely

during one of my trips home years afterwards, I went to the loft for a jar of pickles when my gaze was drawn towards a dusty box with the word 'toys' written on it in thick blue marker; I scrubbed the dust off with my sleeve, blew once or twice, and opened it: dolls with blinking eyes, dominoes (only half a box left), a few children's books with creased edges

there, at the very bottom of the box, was the matchbox house;

it had fallen apart; pijo and penda were buried under a thick layer of dust and the thread had frayed and was no longer connecting them

there was nothing left to keep them together

I wonder what happened to that armchair. Every item bears traces of the people who used it, as a collection of their lives.

My mother liked to sit in the armchair and knit. She used to knit scarves, sweaters, cardigans, even a dress. Every evening after dinner she would sink into the armchair in front of the TV, watching a film while knitting monotonously.

Looking back, it seems like an attempt to knit an invisible cloak to cover all three of us and protect us. With every loop she was entwining the hope that the evening would not go the wrong way.

Sometimes her magic worked.

I was woken by the bang of a slamming door; the three of us were sleeping in the bedroom; my mum, my sister and I; dad had not come home by the time I went to bed; when I opened my eyes, the first thing I that caught my attention was a fire on the balcony; only then did I recognize his silhouette

my father used to smoke a lot but never inside; did he burn something by accident? he stood there on the other side of the glass door, facing us; in one hand he was holding a sweater and in the other one a lighter; while the sweater was burning, he was looking straight into my mother's eyes, laughing

one by one, he set the balls of yarn on fire; my mother didn't move; she remained in bed, lifted slightly on her elbows, looking at this fiery performance through the glass as if none of it was happening

I haven't seen her knitting since then; I wonder whether her hopes for salvation all went to ashes that night, along with the sweater

There are parts of other people layered over me. There are memories, nightmares and events that I don't want to remember. I wanted to get away from them by leaving my childhood, washing them away just to be with myself.

I understand only now that all these people and events are part of me, and they make me who I am.

§

When I had measles, I had to be quarantined straight away, put away in my room, left to my own toys, books, hiding places, to my itchy skin, to my painful loneliness and the dread that I could not go to my mum's room if I heard her crying for help. I was used to spending the time alone, and yet this time it wasn't my choice, and that was hard to accept. I felt like a prisoner in my own place.

When my mother stopped seeing her girlfriend for a Saturday coffee, when she stopped going for runs in the park and joining gatherings at work, I wonder if she felt the same.

§

Sometimes the rays of the summer sun would wake me up early and caress my face with their warmth; it would feel like a loving hand placed over my head, like a smile inviting me to a beautiful day.

It would take a few seconds, a crack in the universe, when time stops; a brief moment of oblivion, like a pocket of safety, before it all came back to me.

– bogdan, go to the head teacher's office immediately!

the maths teacher said

and we all hushed at our desks

we were in year three or four; bogdan was short and slim, but no one dared to touch him; he had no father, but he had an older brother, who, according to the rumours crawling along the corridors at school, was often in the police station for antisocial behaviour; we didn't understand what antisocial behaviour meant, but we kept away from bogdan, just in case

when he came back from the head teacher's office, there were red fingerprints on his face, his ears were glowing

– why did the head teacher call you?

we asked, but he didn't say a word

– perhaps for antisocial behaviour

someone suggested, and so the new rumours began, this time about bogdan himself

after school, I waited for bogdan on the street; when I saw him approaching, I jumped out of the corner where I was hiding, and started hitting him

– you're bad!

I screamed like an animal

I was kicking his ankles, punching his face with my tiny fists, pulling his hair; he was trying to get away, but he didn't hit me back, not even once

– why am I bad?

he asked calmly when I gave up and was about to leave

– I have no idea

I replied, and ran away

in the evening, when bogdan's mother came back from work and

found him scrunched up on the sofa, his tiny body covered in bruises,
she lost her temper

– who did this to you?

she questioned him for hours but bogdan didn't tell

a neighbour, however, had seen me and ratted on me; in the morning, his mother called my dad and told him everything

after school, my father waited for me at the gate; I quickly figured out why; he called to me and bogdan, made me apologize to him and promise to never hit other people again; I apologized; I promised; I really was sorry; I had no idea where that rage had come from; my father was silent on the way home; as soon as we got there, he hissed through his teeth

– nothing will come of you!

When I was angry at the world, I slammed the door behind me and sank into my loneliness.

When I was angry at the world, I killed the fish in the aquarium.

When I was angry at the world, I went to the beach. The sea was beautiful in the winter, looking somewhat angry, blue-green, devoid of all the kitsch that comes along with the summer heat, the shiny bodies inviting the sun, coated in sand and lust. I loved to sit there, looking at the waves and letting my anger merge with them, feeling myself being carried away, far away. Only there was I in harmony with the sea, in harmony with myself.

My mouth waters when I think of the chewing gum 'love is…' I unwrap it impatiently and inhale the banana or strawberry flavour, eyes closed; I unfold the strip, look at the cartoon and read the quote: love is… home, where your heart is; love is… the little things he does for you; love is… what you've created; I collect the strips and place them in a box, my love is… box

if my mum asked me to go to the shop for bread and milk five days a week, the change was enough to get two chewing gum strips on friday, one for me, one for my sister; I always wanted things to be fair; a book for me and for her, new shoes for me and for her, chocolate kuma lisa for me and for her (although she would eat hers while I was keeping mine to enjoy it for longer and I'd find out a few days later that she'd had mine too, so there was nothing left to enjoy)

when I did something wrong, something very bad, such as forgetting to wash my plate after lunch, or if my brand new shoes got covered in mud, my father would punish me by taking all my favourite things away, like opening my chocolate in front of me, eating it slowly, closing his eyes and groaning with pleasure; I would have to look, to remain at the table in front of him and watch

another time he took the chewing gum strips just when I had managed to buy two from the weekly shopping change; he put them both in his mouth and started chewing and making smacking sounds; I was staring at his mouth, following his movements, imagining the sweet taste, which I now had to wait for until next friday

and only if I was good

Bleeding Lane

As I am chopping carrots and beets for a vegetarian borscht, the knife edge slips and leaves a red line on my left thumb. A sting. I don't rush to stop the flow. I stare at the cut; it seems deep. The knife is still in my hand, its blade reflecting the sunlight on the wall. The edge is flirting with my pale skin while I trace the vein up my wrist. The *what if* question stabs my thoughts. It would only take a moment.

– Is dinner ready, Mama? Ka's voice interrupts.

– Almost, I reply, and drop the knife.

I turn on the tap and put my hand underneath the cold running water; the stream changes from clear to pink. I dry it but the cut opens again. With my right thumb I press the cut and hold it for a few seconds. This seems to help. I look around. The carrots look like the beets, all red vegetables lying on the wooden board. Red blobs on the worktop, on the towel and on my white shirt. I reach for the first-aid box in the top drawer and wrap the finger in a plaster.

I throw the vegetables away, clean the top and wash my skirt with soap and cold water, as my mother used to do. The bleeding has stopped, it seems, but a dull pain is still present, underneath the plaster, deep in the bone.

– stop the bleeding, mum; it's running down my legs, I'm dying

– you're not dying, my girl, you're becoming a woman; don't you remember what I told you before; that one day you will become a woman, you will bleed every month for a few days, it will hurt you a little, but it's all right because every woman bleeds like this; don't you remember?

– I didn't know that being a woman meant pain, mum, I didn't know

I bled every night, but no one saw my wounds; I was a child, I hardly understood what was going on

– you won't remember when you grow up

adults said to me

– everything will pass

but I still didn't know how to stop the bleeding

was this my blood?

– How are you feeling today?
   – Like a raw cut; oozing.

I must have been eleven; it was the summer of 1989, a few months before the collapse of communism; the school's head teacher had selected me to go to a summer camp preparing kids to be class captains, developing great leaders, obeying the red party principles; we were going to become pioneers, which meant joining the youth organization led by the party, so it was a big deal to be selected for the camp; I had no intention of becoming a captain, but, knowing my parents, it was my only chance of going anywhere without them, and so I agreed

during the mornings we participated in activities, marched under the blistering sun, studied speeches and prepared a recital for the last night; in the afternoons, we played netball and from time to time we were taken in groups to the beach

when the evenings settled in, we gathered on the square by the canteen, the safe space surrounded by bungalows and the teachers' gaze, strictly overseen in case there was any misconduct; the dj played music for us

we stood together in groups, the girls on one side, the boys on the other; we were giggling, whispering into each other's ears and blushing every time a boy gathered his courage to approach us and invite one of the girls to dance; the girl he'd been following from afar during the day

I can still picture it: a slow ballad starts playing, he approaches, asks you to dance, you leave your giggle in the corner next to the cardigan hanging over the bench, your look becomes serious, exquisite; you don't know how to hold a boy, how to stay that close to a male body, how to dance without stepping on his toes, but you look around, copy the older girls and pretend to know what you're doing; your heart is palpitating, you feel his rapid breathing on your neck, a teacher whistles to remind everyone not to get too close to one another, no intimacy allowed, no inappropriate movements; you dance, move together, and nothing else matters

the boys invited everyone but me; I stood there, alone, like an old tree; the longest blues in my life, the one I never danced

when I woke up in the morning, I found a bright red stain on the sheet; we were six girls in a room; I was horrified but the others, figuring out what was going on, started laughing at me

– congratulations!

they said

– what for? I don't know what to do!

– go buy yourself some cotton from the pharmacy; you'll need a lot of it

it was the ninth of september, a big day for the red party; the camp was about half an hour's drive from the city, so all the parents came to take us home for the day, to celebrate with our families; we had to be returned to the camp by dinner time; I couldn't wait to see mum, but it was only my father in the car; I said hi and remained silent until we got home; the second I stepped in, I ran towards my mother

– I'm bleeding, mum, I'm dying!

when my father overheard, he left the room so as not to bother us women

In the beginning, Milo would buy me big bouquets of flowers for my birthday, along with a special present. He would surprise me with what I'd mentioned I wanted months ago, and I believed I mattered to him.

Later, the gift would be something he'd snatched on his way back from work, and perhaps a bunch of flowers.

Then, just flowers.

two conversations

– *mum, why don't you leave my father?*
  – *because I love him*
  – *but he doesn't deserve to be loved*
  – *everyone deserves to be loved*
  – *is this what love is, mum?*

mum, why don't you leave my father?
  – look at all the flowers he brings me; the other men only buy flowers on international women's day, or birthdays, and he gives me flowers with or without an occasion
  – there's always an occasion, mum; to forgive him for the night before
  at home, we had lots of vases because my father used to buy mum flowers often

I join a group of women who have suffered domestic violence whether recently, or as children. We meet once a week and narrate our shame, anger and fear, trying to connect the words when all we have is emotions, almost impossible to pin down.

The group is like modern medicine, treating the symptoms, dealing with the consequences without looking at the reasons why. Why these men abuse their wives and children, where their violence comes from, how they could be helped in the first place. We sit in a circle, tired eyes, clenched fingers, detached, trying to pacify our dismay and one day, maybe one day, start afresh.

Often, while listening to a woman, another one starts crying, her body shaking, her eyes engulfed in fear.

– I don't want to go back there, she says.

Often, we won't see her again.

Less often I cry too, I but keep going. It's both somewhat soothing and nerve-wracking to know there are others like me out there, like a safety net we've woven without ever realizing.

While attending the group sessions, I come to a realization about the sheer number of women or ex-children, now grown-up women like me, who are damaged, insecure, seeking love in all the wrong places. Sharing our stories doesn't solve anything, but it's a way to untangle things, to understand the unthinkable, to expose our wounded memories and help to heal the past that has been haunting us for years, finding its way and settling in our moments of insomnia.

Along with our own nightmares, we leave the sessions with the stories of others too; with their wounds, their fears, but also with their hopes. We hear about someone else's past reduced to a few sentences in between the weeping, then the story dies down in silence. We carry them within us like unborn babies, they grow bigger and bigger and, although hidden from the outside world, constantly remind us that we've survived, that we are alive. We dream of the ending of these stories, we perform our rituals at new moons to demonstrate our wishes and imagine our new, beautiful lives, our healed minds, our collective future.

in the moonlight his face looks black; only his eyes are glowing, like cats' eyes; they are the only thing you can see of him; the rest is darkness, the rest is the shadows of the trees on the street, dark shadows

the dark circles under my mother's eyes are deep, her face is wrinkled; she has grown old while waiting for my father's fist to land on her cheekbone; his fist is hanging over her like a falcon

the night has faded away, changing its texture and thickness to a lucent veil; she's waiting, not daring to breathe; the evening chill has fallen over the bushes; she will also fall in these bushes in a moment, but now the hand is above her; she will lie there until she freezes, or until someone finds her and helps her to get up, to go on, to keep breathing

this moment is frozen in time now; I see things that are about to happen but I can't do anything; how could I, I am only seven, he is twenty-seven, strong, his mouth stinks of alcohol and dirty words for my mother, and I cover my ears with my hands so I can't hear them

I wish I could scream for help but fear stabs my tongue; I scramble around for words but find nothing; I open my mouth and I stutter; I attempt a sentence and my thoughts dangle; it will take hours before I can replenish my stash of vocabulary

only a moment later his fist will fall over her; it will break her face and the whole world will crumble; please, god, I whisper, keep my mum alive, keep her, please, but there is no reply; it's quiet at this time of night, people are sleeping, the night is sleeping and no one comes to help; they sleep or pretend not to hear, because it's a family matter, it's not their place to interfere

my mother lies in the bushes; the branches have scratched her face; the moon is licking her wounds

Anna is one of the women attending the sessions. She moved here from Spain when she was twenty-four, found some guy who promised to love her for the rest of his life, got married and a year later had her first baby. At thirty-two, she had no job and three children, one boy and two girls. Her husband started beating her soon after she became pregnant with the first one. Something got into him, she said. Every time, he said he loved her and did it to protect her from others. Also, that if she left him one day, he would find her and kill her. So she kept her mouth shut. She bought cheap food and expensive make-up to bury his traces. When she was pregnant with the third one, a midwife noticed the livid marks on her back. She gave her a note with a free number to call for help. So she did. It took her eight years. She was first welcomed at a refuge centre, then moved to a different city where they helped her to find a job and start her life afresh.

That was a few years ago. She is happy now, she is telling us jokes. Sometimes she starts weeping when a new woman joins the group.

Anna and I decide to go for a walk one weekend. We aren't sure if we are supposed to tell the rest, or whether we are even allowed to see each other outside the sessions, but no one has told us otherwise, so we meet at Hackney Wick station and go for a walk by the canal-side. It's a beautiful afternoon, so lively in this part of the city with all the people around: some passing by on bikes, others sitting on beach chairs drinking beer or trendy vegan smoothies, and the lucky owners of the boats repairing, painting, preparing their homes on water for the colder months to come.

One of the boats is a floating cafe, so we grab a latte and sit on the lawn opposite. The woman, a hippy-looking lady in a low-cut red vest and a long flowery skirt, brings us a couple of floor cushions, plays Manu Chao and turns the volume up slightly. We soak up the good vibes, feeling comfortable in each other's presence without the need to speak.

– I started dating again, you know, she says, breaking the silence.

– That's great, Anna. Anyone in particular?

– Yeah, there's this guy, Anthoan. A nice guy, works for a charity. Doesn't have children but seems to be fine with looking after mine. He's one of five siblings so he's used to lots of kids in the family, you know. We might have one or two babies together.

She laughs.

– Isn't that a bit too soon for you?

– Soon? Why? I need someone, you know. Someone to love, someone to be around, to cook dinner for, to make me feel secure.

– But you didn't feel secure with your ex-husband, right?

– No, but it's different now.

– How do you know?

– I know because Anthoan is different. He's kind to me, he has strong hands, buys me flowers.

I let her words fill my head. I look up, close my eyes and give myself to the beams of sunshine caressing my face. I imagine this man, Anthoan. I imagine his strong hands, his naked brown arms, his smell of coffee the morning after. He reminds me of someone, but I cannot figure out whom. Someone distant, like a dark shadow, perhaps someone I've loved but never knew I did.

– And the sex is amazing, she says, her voice interrupting my thoughts.

– The sex, yeah.

I sip the coffee and bite my lip, trying hard not to say anything further to spoil her joy. The truth is, none of us can be sure of what's right; whether jumping into a new relationship so soon after the end of a traumatic one is a good or a bad thing. No one knows if this Anthoan is the right guy for her either. But she is taking the plunge. She likes it this way; she wants to try.

I take another sip and close my eyes again. This time I wish I were as brave as her.

mum is an only child, no brothers and sisters; my grandmother is the youngest of five sisters, and each of the other four has two kids, meaning my mother has eight first cousins; they all got married, had children, and now I have sixteen uncles and aunts

one of my aunts once gave me a silver key to keep as an amulet; she said that keys brought luck to aquarians; my aunt wished me well and wanted me to be safe and happy; I knew this, so I put the silver key on a leather string and wore it as a necklace, so it would always be with me

at the end of the summer, a friend asked me to go with her to an evangelist church; she said she wished me well and wanted to help me, so I went along; there, men and women praised god with songs, then they received the holy spirit and spoke strange words I could not understand

at the end of the service, the priest walked among the people with a box where everyone had to donate what they could afford; I had no change on me; the silver key was my most valuable object; it was my only hope for salvation, and the only chance of making everything right at home

later, when my father found out where I'd been, he banned me from going anywhere near that church, as well as from seeing my friend

– churches are for people getting married; no other reason to go there he made his point clear

I had to obey; either way, I had nothing else to donate, no change to spare, no hope to keep

We never got married, Milo and I, not officially, at least. But what turns a relationship into a marriage? Is it the common things, accumulated with time, the quiet evenings together, the arguments, the empty toothpaste tubes, the emptiness between us on the sofa?

Our relationship turned into friction between two people leading separate lives while inhabiting the same space. Thinking about it now, perhaps I wasn't ready to move our relationship forward and build a family together. We started arguing more and more. But, at the same time, I was indulging myself by believing in his continuing affection towards me, as only a fucked-up mind, a child who grew up with an abusive parent, could do.

Perhaps that was the beginning of the end.

the first man in my life, before any other man, before any other love,
was my father

    my father, who I had and didn't have, who I wanted to love but
didn't know how; no one showed me how to love a man

    I still don't know

To-do list found in an old notebook:

1. Buy bread and a (small) piece of cheese
2. Smile and embrace the day
3. Embrace Mum when she's back from work
4. Wash my clothes
5. Wash away the feeling of rage one day. And forgive

§

The desire to arrange objects and things in my life is supplanted by apathy, which, like a straw in a glass of orange juice, stirs my day; the particles spin around and chaos fills my existence. I get up late in the morning, late to take Ka to the nursery, late for work, and drag myself out of bed, rough and shaggy, leaving everything behind, Tracey Emin-style, as a rebellion against my own broken life.

at the same time as my father went to do military training for a month, the supermarket started stocking this new delicious vanilla cream in ceramic bowls

– such lovely bowls

my mum said, and every friday after work she bought a couple: one for me, one for my sister

we ate the vanilla cream, its silky sweetness dancing over our tongues, then she washed the bowls and placed them in the glass cupboard in the kitchen; by the end of the month she had assembled a complete set

the saturday before dad came back, mum got the bowls out and lined them up on the worktop

– what are you planning to do with them?

I asked

– you'll see

she opened her recipe book and started placing products next to the bowls

she began by breaking the eggs one by one into a big glass container and whisking them with a mixer; then, she added sugar, half a cup, and finally poured some milk; I stood next to her holding my doll, watching her moves and absorbing the magic

I followed each step of the recipe along with mum; I took a pinch of her smile, added the serenity of this saturday afternoon, stirred everything with an imaginary wooden spoon in an imaginary glass container, and finally poured the mixture into a few imaginary bowls; together, we made such a delicious crème brûlée

I so desperately wanted to be like mum

and I was so desperately trying never to become like her

STOP NINE
Silent Garden

The silence between me and Milo was steadily growing bigger and bigger, taking up the space for the conversations we used to have.

§

A phone call, from my sister. Before I picked up the phone, I already knew what she would say.

– Father died.

I didn't say a word. I hung up quietly, so as not to disturb the silence.

§

I didn't go.

They sent him off quickly, in a DIY coffin, my mum told me later. There were five or six people and a drunken gravedigger. They forgot to include the notebook containing poems he had written for my mother and the printed photos of me and my sister. From his grave one could see the shores of the beach.

He would have liked the view.

§

My daughter, while I'm brushing her hair in the morning in front of the mirror:

– Mama, when you become a granny, who will be my mama then?

– I will always be your mama, baby.

– Even when you die?

§

If one day I am diagnosed with a terminal disease and I know I only have weeks or months to live, I won't write letters to my daughter for when she is older. I know what pain is.

I would want her to say goodbye to me once and then to embrace life. I would, of course, like the idea of her keeping me inside, remembering me and letting me see the world through her. But I wouldn't want to be the ghost that's haunting her in moments when she is the happiest and remind her of her loss, again and again, as a punishment for living when her mother is not. I would do everything possible for pain to elude her.

§

Father's will did not exist, not as a legal document at least, and yet I still carry its weight.

My sister has taken everything from my mother: the almond-shaped eyes, the right nose, the well-defined full lips and the golden-blonde hair. Mum also bestowed upon her the patience to knit and embroider. Also, my sister is trying to fit into that emerald-green blouse that my mother used to wear in high school.

She's snatched her silver earrings and the almost-never-worn platform shoes. One day the whole flat will be bequeathed to my sister.

I have taken everything from my father: the big nose, the green eyes and the fiery temper. That's all. That was all he had.

as children, my sister used to wear my old clothes when I grew out
of them
    – there is still life in them
    she liked to say
    she enjoyed dressing up like me, feeling like me, being like me; I saw
her kissing my ex-boyfriend once in his father's garage when I happened
to walk by; I didn't blame her, or him; he couldn't get over me for
ages; perhaps he had met her and she reminded him of our old times;
perhaps he felt a bit nostalgic but, knowing there was no chance of
us getting back together, hit on my sister, like finding a substitute, or
that's what I liked to think
    – there was still life in him
    she confessed years later
    I wished she had said she just wanted to be me

When I went to my father's grave the following summer, instead of flowers, I left a handful of empty shells.

How many times did the sea drag me down? I'd swallow the water, its salty taste. It would fill me up, it would run through my veins, until I became the sea itself.

My dad was that sea now: one moment stormy, the next calm and serene.

I dropped the hollow shells near the wooden cross, just below his picture.

§

The last time I saw my father, he had no money, no front teeth and no wedding ring. The teeth he lost in an argument with someone on the street that evolved in the wrong direction, and the wedding ring he sold to a pawnshop to buy new teeth, but the money was not enough, so instead he bought some bread and salami, as well as a bottle of cognac.

The last time I saw my father, we smoked a lot and talked a little. When we emptied my box of cigarettes, I went to the store for some more and came back with a full plastic bag of food. I gave it to him and he couldn't believe his eyes. He found it hard to accept food from me, and hard to carry the heavy bag back to the basement where he was living temporarily after my mother had finally left him. He had lost a lot of weight but couldn't afford to lose his dignity, so I said that the food I'd bought for him was with money he had lent me some time ago.

I left and immediately felt guilty. On the way back, I kept thinking how I would explain to my mother that I'd just helped my father while betraying her.

§

My aunt, Dad's sister, asked me to go to her place and collect his belongings.

– He didn't have much, she said.

It was an old shoebox containing our family photos, a few CDs with his favourite music, a notebook. Underneath all this, I found a letter from me. It was the one I'd sent him a couple of weeks before he died. I opened it and started reading it through blurred vision, hearing my own voice and imagining how he must have felt reading it. It was a blend of rage and blame, but at the very bottom of it, there was a soup recipe, followed by one final sentence: 'Try to eat well and take care of yourself.' Was I ready to forgive him? Was that the beginning of a reconciliation that never happened, since he had abruptly vanished into nothing?

The memories appeared much like the letter in my hands, eroded by friction, folded and tucked into a pocket. That piece of paper was like a road map of my journey, a testimony of my decision to leave, starting from the dark corners of my childhood, travelling miles and crossing borders, mainly personal, to arrive at a present where I thought I would be safe, a place where I thought I would find salvation.

– None of this belongs to me any more. You can either keep it or throw it away; it's your choice, I told my aunt, and left.

§

Another phone call; this time it was about my grandma.

I bought a plane ticket right away and packed my black dress in the bag.

§

My mother:

– I have so many knitted table runners left from your grandmother, stacks, piles of them, knitted with a crochet hook, with two arthritic hands, with a lot of heart. What am I going to do with all these knitted table runners now, how am I going to fill their holes…

§

– I don't want to be a burden to you, said Grandma once and, bent in two, she dug her head into the wardrobe and started taking out all the towels, dresses and bed linen, hoarded for years.

– This linen bed set was my trousseau for the wedding. The orange flowery dress too, she murmured to herself.

She ran her fingers slowly over the fabric, as if caressing the memories of her youth, and put the trousseau back in the wardrobe. Everything else, neatly folded, she placed in transparent plastic bags.

– I will give them to the gypsy woman, the one that comes to wash the stairs on Wednesday, she said.

When we buried her, her body was light as a feather. When she left, her soul took all her weight away and crushed it over the space left by her absence. Then the whole village ate boiled barley with plain tea biscuits, walnuts and icing sugar. The sugar covered the barley in the plastic bowls, white and fluffy as the sadness that had just sprinkled our heads. Then it melted away in the toothless mouths of the elderly women, but it felt glued to the back of mine.

On the grave we planted white daisies, like those she used to grow in her garden. Their leaves were so fine and frail. The wind pounded them, and they trembled. In the clarity of the air after rain, their whiteness seemed even more pristine, just like my grandma's face before they closed the coffin.

When we came back the next day, there was nothing left of the daisies. The local goats had eaten them, to the last stalk. Mum became so upset.

It doesn't matter any more, I thought.

– We'll plant new ones and we'll ask the gravediggers to lock the gate in the evening, I said to her.

§

Coming back from the therapy session, on the bus, I look at Ka. She seems so delicate, glancing through the window, four already but her thumb still finds refuge in her mouth every time she needs to comfort herself. I wonder how much she has overheard from the conversations we have, how much she has understood of all the things I've said, and how much she sensed what remained unsaid. She is my daughter and I think I know her so well, and yet she is another person. I look at her; her face seems a bit tense examining the buildings and the people we pass by, and I wonder what she's thinking right now. I feel her somehow drifting away from me, as if a glass wall is placed between us and I can observe but can't hear or change anything on the other side.

I think about my mother and how she probably thought she knew me well too, how she thought she knew what was best for me. I would often hear her say that she was staying with my father because of me and my sister, that if it wasn't for us, she would have left him by then. The feeling of guilt was creeping slowly and permeated me permanently like the invisible damp in the room that you can feel but can never get rid of.

Back then, the thought that I might have been the reason for my pregnant mother first to marry him, and then to stay with him despite the daily abuse, might not have been fully formed in my fragile mind, but its pressure had subsequently grown bigger and bigger and had filled me up.

Ka interrupts my thoughts:

– Mama, how many days until my birthday?

– Let me see… Twenty-one. Why?

– Can I choose my present?

– Don't you prefer it to be a surprise?

– I do, so you can still surprise me with it.

– OK, what is it then?

– Can I have Daddy home for a sleepover, please?

It's our stop. The moment we get off the bus and walk down the street, it starts raining, heavy drops, pouring over us, over our long hair, over my face.

§

– Dinner is in the fridge, you just need to warm it up. Ka goes to bed at seven thirty, she likes listening to a bedtime story, there are plenty of books on the shelf in her room, just pick one. Make sure she brushes her teeth before bed. Ah, and no TV, please.

I give instructions to the babysitter I hired from the Nannies by the Hour website. She looks about twenty years old, and I am itching to ask her if she's ever cared for young children before, but the site claims they check the nannies and, besides, I am running late, so I abandon the idea.

– Don't worry about a thing, madam.

She smiles at me reassuringly, as if reading my thoughts.

– We'll be fine, like, really no need to fret. Go out and enjoy yourself.

Getting used to leaving Ka with strangers for the evening is not easy. I find the whole experience distressing, mostly for me, less so for her, but I'm determined to give it a chance. I'm going out with a friend from work; he has a spare ticket for a contemporary dance show at the Barbican after his boyfriend cancelled last minute. It's a local production with international appeal, he said. The plan is to eat something on the go, watch the show, then finish the night with a few drinks. I can't help but check my phone every few minutes, in case the babysitter has texted with a question or, in the worst-case scenario, with an emergency. She hasn't.

We take our places and the show begins. It's a hybrid performance between a film shown on-screen and real-time dance onstage. It starts with the film, showing a neighbourhood. It looks like a deprived area where men walk in groups, hide in dark corners, slip into shadows. They follow a man down the street, they run after him, catch him, start punching him like wild animals. The man lies on the street; the rest are stomping over his body, their faces twisted in anger. The camera moves the focus to a hand, holding a knife. I almost manage to stop thinking about Ka at home, immersing myself in the show.

The screen goes black and the spotlight moves to the corner of the stage, where the same man from the film lies, not moving. Other men come onstage. There are many of them. A sudden roar. The strong brown bodies start stomping in rage; they rise up against the act of violence, a powerful contrast with society's racist prejudice against people of colour. The man gets up slowly, turns towards the audience and looks at me, straight into my eyes. I feel uneasy but look back at him. There is something about that face that brings back memories.

Later that night in bed, after a few cocktails and scrambled thoughts, I catch myself thinking of Kyron. I imagine him dancing onstage, his body moving, his eyes catching mine, as though he were dancing just for me and for that very moment.

– what's wrong with you today?

my dance teacher, miss ivanova, asks me

she is standing in front of me, demanding an answer, some sort of apology for my clumsy moves and lack of attention

– miss, I… I'm all right

I mutter

– then go back into first position and focus, girl

I join the other girls; we move from positions one to five, followed by a series of demi-pliés, but when I attempt to do a pas de chat, I faint and fall on the floor; the girls start laughing at me

– you have to tell me what's going on

miss ivanova lowers her voice while helping me get up

– I can't dance today, miss, I'm sorry; it's my back

– your back? what are you, a granny?

– it hurts, miss

– why, what happened? did you fall?

– no… my father, he…

– quiet! be quiet, girls!

– my father came back drunk last night; he entered my room while I was doing my homework and started shouting at me for not having finished by then; then…

– enough!

she replies with frustration, then grows quiet

with my peripheral vision I see her staring at me with fear and disgust, as if my words are spreading an infection, some deadly illness from which she wants to spare herself

I didn't say anything further; I didn't tell her how he shouted in my face, nor about the smell of alcohol getting into my nostrils, the punches to my hips, the stabbing pain that remained *my attempt to tell someone was cut short, so I didn't see the point of trying ever again*

people were afraid to know; I was afraid of the silence

– Mama, what is death?
  – Why are you asking, Ka?
  – I want to know.
  – It's the beginning and the end.
  – What ends and what begins, Mama?
  – What ends rebirths and starts again. It's called life.
  – So death means life?

§

– How do you feel about your father's death?
  – What do you want me to say? Relieved? See, the end is never really the end. There's no sudden door slamming, no end of the road, and sometimes, not even a coffin slumping into the ground. Often, the end is the beginning of something new.

§

My father's death was not the death of my father. Not an end. Maybe just an initial illusion of something approaching closure.

He is with me all the time, even more often now than before. Every time I see echoes of him around me, I relive my memories, all the traumatic experiences. Recently, in addition to the feeling of fear, new questions have emerged and clung to me. Was it all his fault? Did he have a reason to behave the way he did? Perhaps a feeling of guilt for not being willing or able to understand him earlier, too.

§

Water is like a card's magnetic strip, I learn from a TV documentary. It has memory and keeps information about everything it has come into contact with, everything it's passed through on its way to the tap. Scientists have carried out an experiment and proved that if you whisper beautiful words to a glass of water, it changes its structure and forms beautiful crystals. If you're angry and shout ugly words, the crystals also create ugly shapes like rotten wood. And, because the human body is composed of about seventy per cent water, the same thing happens to us.

I imagine the crystals in my body: shapeless, asymmetrical, black. When I drink water, I remember to whisper beautiful words into the glass. Love. Strength. Beginning.

*music also causes water to form beautiful crystals; especially classical
music*

*in primary school no one loved our music teacher; I remember how
we had to stand in front of the whole class, how he made us sing the
notes while measuring the beat with a stick on his desk; every time one
of us sang out of tune or out of rhythm, the stick changed its direction
and dropped onto the head of the singing child; we left our music classes
with a terrible headache, which went on for days, often until music
class the following week*

*that morning a young woman came in, who introduced herself as
our new music teacher; there were rumours that one of our classmate's
headaches had got worse; her parents took her to the doctor, and she
was forced to tell both the doctor and her terrified parents all about the
music classes, the stick and the teacher's habit of disciplining us; the
next day after school, the father waited for the music teacher outside
the gates and smashed his cheekbones*

the music teacher never returned; neither did our classmate

When we grew up, the five-year difference between my sister and me melted away, along with the chubbiness of our faces. We hadn't seen each other since I'd left the country; our grandma's funeral gathered us in one place, as if she had planned it on purpose. In the evening, we sat next to each other on the bed with our knees jutting out in the dark like cranes left on a building site. We talked for hours.

– Do you remember that time when they took us to the funfair and you fell off the carousel?

– I remember the fair. Daddy won a teddy bear from the shooting stall, and we argued over it the whole way back home, she replied.

– What are you talking about! We never argued.

– What are *you* talking about! We always quarrelled, she said, ending the conversation.

I'm sure we're both right. That both events happened at the same time; one through my eyes, the other through hers. As we were sitting in the dark, leaning against the wall, silence settled between us. I often wonder what our childhood looked like from her side of the bed.

§

Before he developed his love for cognac, my father was a child and loved eating all sorts of sweets. One day after school he took the five-leva note left on the kitchen shelf, went to a nearby bakery and bought a whole tray of sweet, syrupy tulumbi. He placed the tray on a table, sat in the chair and didn't leave until had finished them all, to the salesman's astonishment.

In the evening, when his parents heard the story from the

bakery man and then found out that the five-leva note was missing, they quickly worked things out and got very angry.

– Why did you steal the money? they asked my seven-year-old father.

– I didn't steal it; I found it on the shelf.

They didn't find this funny. Bad kids need to be punished, they said. Otherwise, bad kids become bad people. That's what they said and left him there, standing by the wall with his arms raised and a full, aching stomach, for the rest of the night.

§

There's no such thing as closure. There is no way to forget. But there are continuations, departures and arrivals. Perhaps, one day, there will be forgiveness too.

§

When we were little, my sister and I didn't laugh much. We would play quietly in our room, trying not to make any noise, so that we didn't disturb our parents and make them angry with us. They had their own troubles and didn't need more.

Now, as grown-ups, with the past behind us, we laugh every time we get together. We are loud and unafraid of showing joy. We sit in the room, arms touching, the door wide open so that we let our laughter travel far.

§

A year after my father's death, on the exact date, I bought a tray of tulumbi and gave them all to my neighbours, 'for God's forgiveness'. When I explained, people were surprised at this strange ritual, but thanked me and took the tulumbi, salivating already. They were nice tulumbi, freshly baked, sweet, syrupy, just the way my father liked them.

The day that marked two years after his passing, I bought a tray of tulumbi again, but this time, instead of giving them away to the neighbours, I ate them all. I forced myself to finish the whole lot to the very last crumb. I felt sick but kept eating. I had to find a way to get to the end. And also, to find a way to forgive him.

At last, I threw up and, feeling cleansed and empty, I started afresh.

§

I watched her piling the food on her plate, not skipping a single dish from the buffet.

– For £6.90 you can eat as much as you can fit in, she said when she noticed my gaze, despite me trying to hide my astonishment. And right now my stomach can fit quite a lot. Yours too, by the way, she continued, nodding towards my almost empty plate. Are you planning to live on salads?

– I'm not hungry, I replied.

– Everything is linked to stress. You need to meditate more. I find yoga exercises super relaxing. But they also make me ravenous. She winked and shoved a slice of ham in her mouth.

We met in pregnancy yoga classes. It turned out that our due dates were both in August, just five days apart. She decided that we must become friends and go for walks in the park with the prams when the babies were born.

In the yoga classes, a dozen heavily pregnant women tried to reach their toes from a sitting position, but we could barely reach our knees; we puffed and panted, and finally gave up.

The yoga instructor's voice reached me:

– Don't forget about your breathing. Inhale, one, two, hold, exhale, three, four...

We then lay on the mats, exhausted, with our eyes closed. We would breathe positive energy in and breathe the negative thoughts out. We were meditating on the umbilical cord and building a strong connection with our unborn babies.

That was years ago, but I still practise it from time to time.

I breathe in deeply and then exhale forever.

§

My hope of one day feeling safe and free was never fulfilled.

The presence of my father's absence was inhabiting the air I was inhaling, growing bigger and bigger. Inhale, one, two, three…

§

– How are you feeling today?
  – Is this a question?

STOP TEN
Mother's Gate

I didn't know how it would feel to become a mother even when my waters broke with a gush in the middle of the night. A strong cramping, followed by a dragging heaviness, had crept into my lower back earlier that evening and lingered there for hours, but I had decided to ignore it. As I scrambled to the bathroom, I noticed fluid dripping down my legs, leaving a dotted trail on the wooden floor. I knew from the pregnancy books that the amniotic fluid was supposed to be pale yellow and clear, but the colour of mine was red. I was horrified. I rushed back to our bedroom.

– Wake up, Milo! Get up, quickly. My waters have broken.
He looked confused.
– Is the baby coming?
When he noticed the bloodstains all over the bed linen, he jumped out of bed and called the hospital. He was trying to come across as calm and collected, but his voice was trembling. The midwife wanted to speak to me, he said, she wanted to hear my breathing.

I couldn't talk, couldn't breathe. I was frozen, as though seeing the worst coming before it had happened. I grabbed my hospital bag and the car keys and we dashed into the darkness. It was 1 a.m.; the roads were empty, just a few taxis driving in the night. I tried to stay focused, to observe my breathing, my contractions that had suddenly appeared, but I was still feeling weak, like an echo.

When we arrived at the hospital and the midwife examined me, I was three centimetres dilated. Because my waters had broken, she attached me to a machine and put me on a drip with hormones to speed up the labour. The contractions quickly increased in strength and frequency. There was no comfortable position. I wanted to snuggle down but I also couldn't stay in bed. The midwives in their dark blue tunics were bruising the sterile whiteness of the ward. The pain was coming and fading as ocean waves down my back and wrapping around my bump.

I thought of the Black Sea, the way I remembered it from my childhood: stormy, roaring, dark green in those late autumn evenings. I would sit on the bench near the beach, surrounded by no one but seagulls, wrapped in my green coat and long rust-orange scarf, and I would study the rippling waves approaching and crashing on the shore then slowly subsiding back into the water mass only to gain strength and come back with even greater power.

Milo was right beside me in the maternity ward, but I pushed him away when my contractions increased in strength and frequency. He didn't mind; it was my body and my pain, after all. He read the newspaper, made himself instant coffee, had a quick bite in front of the hospital kiosk, napped on the chair in the room, then repeated all of the above and came back just in time to witness Ka's birth.

I was in labour for almost eighteen hours. During all this time, I was fully concentrating on my pain. Not even for a second did I think about the baby. When I finally delivered her and the midwife took her away to be checked, it was the first time I realized that the whole experience was supposed to be about her, not me. I asked if she was OK and they said yes. I glimpsed her tiny red, wrinkled body and sighed in relief, my eyelids suddenly feeling heavy.

The woman in the bed next to mine delivered a baby whose intestines were hanging out of his body. The doctors knew about it in advance, so they performed a C-section and took the baby to theatre to operate on him immediately. The mother would not stop praying for her child, her lips rustling, her face stretched with tension.

Sometimes I feel like my intestines are hanging out of me, leaving an empty space, a deep hole inside, filled with fear.

On the third day, we were discharged and drove back home; this home was both familiar and strange, a place and life we were about to discover. In these first few days, an unsettling feeling had nested in me, a worry that didn't let me sleep at night. How would I keep her away from the evil eye?

towards the end of the winter, the kukeri gather and dance in my grandparents' village; there aren't many places in the country that keep this tradition alive; I know a bit about it, but want to witness it myself, so I go into the village at the weekend

I arrive at the square, where young men have crowded already; one of them, who they call the bride, is dressed in a red dress and bride's veil; another one is called the priest and wears a long black cassock while the rest of the men are hopping around, wearing fur costumes with scary sheepskin masks, copper cowbells hanging on their belts, ringing

they all gather here, in the village centre, have a sip or two of strong rakia to warm up in the january cold, and leave; they jump from foot to foot, their bells rattle rhythmically, and so they go around the village

I recognize a neighbour under his mask and approach him to say hello, but instead of pinching my cheek, as he usually does, he puffs up like a hedgehog and thrusts his mask so close to my face that his look makes me shiver; the other kukeri dancers surround me and start dancing around while the priest calls my name and splashes holy water over me; someone in the crowd reaches my hand and somehow pulls me out of there

— what are you doing, girl? no human being should go near the kukeri!
— but why?

I ask, shocked and puzzled

— why? because they chase the devil! that's their job, to scare everything bad and evil from our village and to chase it far away; keep your distance and let them perform the ritual

I merge with the crowd, along with the others watching from a safe distance, and absorb the sound of the bells; I let myself give in to their dance that chases away the dark forces and cleanses us; I want to believe that their terrifying masks will scare the bad from our home and push it away, far away

I used to dream that the evil would go away, far away.

Falling asleep, I would pray for my life to change one day. I would emigrate in my sleep, morph into a raindrop falling over a distant place. Then, plunging into the earth, I would turn into a flower; the wind would carry my smell to my mother so that she knew I was alive, that I was reborn and waiting to see her again someday, somewhere.

But I was still there and everything was the same, and there was nothing else I could do but clench my teeth.

§

Da–da. These were my daughter's first words when she was around six months old, at the same time her first two front teeth erupted. Not *ma–ma*, as most babies say, but a sonorous, clear *da–da*. I took it personally. I felt almost offended. I gave up my job for you, my sleep for you, my social life for you, and your first words are for him, I would think to myself in despair. But I knew it wasn't personal. Children do whatever they want. Sometimes they can be cruel to their parents without knowing. Other times, parents can be cruel to their children, without realizing it.

§

I liked examining the little face while breastfeeding her: the tiny little mouth, the wide-open blue eyes that pierced mine, the delicate fingers grasping my breast. Sometimes I felt anxious for feeding her my milk, afraid that the toxic thoughts might enter her body, like the codeine I was taking to numb the pain after giving birth.

§

– What did you like about Milo?

– I haven't really thought about it before. I guess he didn't resemble my father.

– Just that?

– That was enough. At first, he helped me build my confidence in a place that was still foreign to me.

– And then?

– And then...

§

For years I hated myself for not being able to play basketball the way my father wanted me to play, that I couldn't write poems the way he wanted me to write, that I had a big nose and wasn't as pretty, humble and obedient as he would have liked me to be.

Today I am that baby he didn't want to be born, the four-year-old child who learned the police phone number before learning to read and count, the seven-year-old girl hiding under the table when he started chasing her mother, the thirteen-year-old girl who knew the taste of her own blood long before she knew the taste of a kiss.

Today I stand in front of myself, the way a little child stands in front of the mirror for the first time and examines herself, takes a good look and learns to discover, to accept and to love.

Today I say to all those kids, each child I was and still am, *everything is fine, don't worry.*

Everything is fine.

§

At home, I grew accustomed to the constant chaos, to the silence settled between us, to Milo's demands of me. I feared that one day I would stop noticing the way we were in our

221

relationship, the way he was with me; and that I would stop noticing my own self.

§

Things seemed pretty normal in the first months after Ka was born, almost fine. Milo went to work and I stayed with the baby; fed her, changed her nappies, took her for a walk in the park, made her laugh, made dinner. He came back tired and everything irritated him, even her sweet gurgling to welcome him home. I rushed to put her to bed, so I could spend the evening with him. He said he loved his daughter but preferred it this way.

– Babies are cutest when they're asleep, he used to joke with our friends.

They smiled with understanding and I smiled too, despite feeling exhausted from my sleepless nights and never-ending breastfeeding.

At nights when she cried, I hurried to comfort her to prevent his shouting at her to shut up. He moved to the spare bedroom so that he could get a good night's sleep. I lost my appetite, my breast milk and my sanity, and started thinking of switching to the bottle, overnight at least. There was pressure from my mum, midwives and the media to go on a little longer, but Milo didn't really care; it was my milk, my breast and my decision, after all.

The less attention he gave to Ka, the more she cried for him, as though creating a magnetic field that only the two of them could understand. At first, I didn't want to pay too much attention to it; he was her father and she needed to bond with him. But over time, I started to feel jealous; to me it felt unfair that she wouldn't recognize me as the person caring for her, doing everything for her. I started feeling isolated, depressed, abandoned by my own child.

Nine months later I was ready to go back to work. I was craving social contact, some sort of recognition that I was more than just a mother. I needed to prove to myself that I was still worth something, that I was able to achieve, to communicate beyond baby talk, and to enjoy myself. My life was on hold, as if I'd pressed the pause button or given it to someone else, or at least that's how I was feeling. I needed it back, and I was ready for it.

§

– Mama, would I die if I jumped from the top of that tall building over there?

– Ka, why would you want to jump? Of course you'd die.

– Well, the teacher, Miss Lewis, said the other day that her cat jumped from the seventh floor of her building; it hurt its tummy but survived.

– That's because cats have nine lives.

– Nine? But how would a cat know it's living the last one?

§

I once read that the child visually most resembles the parent who was the dominant one in the relationship.

After dinner, I help my daughter wash her teeth, shower her, wrap her in a grass-green bath towel, then dress her in her pyjamas and, snuggled up next to her on the bed, read a bedtime story. From time to time, I ask her to try and read the easy words – and, had, me, sun – while I'm reading the rest of it out loud. She is always disappointed when the story ends and it's time for her to sleep, but she drifts off by the time I walk down the stairs to the living room and switch on the baby monitor. It's a video monitor that displays an image. I zoom in and study her face. Her features are soft: rounded face, pellucid skin. But there is something barely noticeable that shows through. Her father.

§

– How do you feel about Ka? Do you love her?

  – What a question! Do you assume I don't love my child because she wasn't planned or because I wanted to terminate the pregnancy at first? Or that I am just like my father, who never wanted me?

  – I don't assume anything.

  – Why do you need to know then?

  – I don't. You do.

§

Love is not something you pour over your child, I've learned that. For some, it works. They start developing the loving from the moment they see their newborn, or even before that, during the time preceding that first meeting, the months of pregnancy. But sometimes it takes time. Where I end, she starts, I used to think. It's only now that I start finding pleasure in caring for Ka, where before I thought of it as a burden.

When do you become a mother? It's not when you expel a baby through the birth canal or through the precise incision under your navel. It's not when you bring her home in the carrycot along with your anxiety that this baby is all *yours*; yours to care for, yours to love, yours to worry about. It's also not when you hold her, crying, in the coffee shop where you've met with a friend and where, despite all efforts to look collected, a feeling of desperation is hemming you in. You become a mother slowly, gradually, in small increments of the everyday clashes with your previous life, in the quiet moments when, feeding her, studying her gentle features, you realize how much she depends on you, how fragile she is, how deeply attached.

I dread everything that is demanded of me so I push it away, leaving it aside for as long as possible. The expectation from people around me that, being a woman, I should want to become a mother, and that once pregnant, I should be feeling excited and looking forward to it, confused me. It was as though their image of normality weighed on me like a stone, not letting me breathe, pressing down my own feelings, crushing down my instinct to be the way I am.

My mum always tried to be the perfect mother, to compensate for the absent, or, rather, negatively present, father in my life. But her drive for personal perfection was also a demand for the same from her children. It created, perhaps, the very first instances of pressure for me to follow her example, to be ambitious for myself and to also expect the same from the world. Paradoxically, this only created a chain of far from perfect events, at the core of them my wrecked, far from perfect self.

Completely detached from my own needs and aiming to obey the rules set by the maternal ideal, I reluctantly started fitting in with the requirements of the role as shaped by society. A society that didn't care for individual women but was only interested in reproduction. I felt trapped within these restrictions and, feeling under pressure, I set out to be the opposite, an example of imperfection. I dreaded making the same mistakes as my mother; I was afraid of loving, being hurt, of disappointments; I cocooned my inner desire to live. Then, swathed and blinded, I went on to make all the wrong choices, be with all the wrong men, take all the wrong paths.

It felt right then; I had my reasons to be the way I was. I feel bad about it now, but there is no way to change the past.

while relaxing on a bench near the beach one summer afternoon, a young man approached me and asked if I minded him sitting next to me; I nodded; he had a wide smile, big white teeth and strong hands; I was fourteen and absent-minded

he took a seat and the closeness made me blush; although I wasn't looking at him, I was feeling his presence and I liked it; he asked me whether I came there often, which school I went to, where I lived; he asked my name and why my eyes were so sad

– why are your hands so strong?

I asked in turn

– to hug you better

he replied, and I flinched

– it's time for me to go

I said, and I sought his hand to shake it goodbye; then I noticed that his trousers were undone and his hand was digging in

I jumped and ran away; I didn't know if he was running after me, but I was too frightened to stop and look back

at home, I locked the door, I locked this event deep inside me, and I promised myself never to talk to strangers ever again

– It wasn't all bad, my father used to say.

I want to recall those sweet moments, the cracks in time when something good had happened to us. I close my eyes and search for those moments hiding in the creases of my memory, trapped by the time that has passed by, locked.

we're on the street, surrounded by thousands of people, all of us march-
ing in lines and rows, wearing flags and flowers, greeting others; it's
one of those may day demonstrations; the whole nation is celebrating
on the streets of every city, town and small village; I am four or five,
too little to walk fast, so my dad is carrying me on his shoulders; from
here, I'm able to see the whole procession, to notice things so far ahead
of me, as if from a bird's vantage point

I wished I could always see a few steps ahead, to glimpse the future
and try to prevent bad things from happening; I imagined myself sitting
on my dad's shoulders and navigating us through the crowd; but things
don't always happen the way we wish them to

I squeeze my eyes shut and try really hard to think of something
else; I am twelve and I have a terrible headache that blurs my vision
and makes me feel sick; I'm lying on the sofa in the living room, eyes
closed, the pain hammering my brain; my father is sitting next to me
looking worried; he is touching my head gently, massaging my forehead,
starting from the base of my eyebrows and moving upwards in slow,
circular movements; his hands feel supple and warm against my skin
– don't worry, everything will be ok soon

I hear him whisper and I don't know if I can trust his words, but I feel
hypnotized and stay still, giving myself up to his touch; the same hand
that slaps the face, the fist that hits, the fingers that pull hair are now
touching me as if nothing has ever happened, as if he loves me indeed

I try hard to remember; but what are memories? Little fragments
flying in the continuum of time, photos scattered on the floor like
broken glass, something borrowed from the past that doesn't fit in the
present and only serves to remind us that it is obsolete

I stand in the middle of all this like a mirror, showing a distorted
reflection of my past

I catch myself still being drawn towards the bad memories and the fear, and open my eyes. Perhaps I will try again another time. There must be good times that I can find somewhere deep in my mind; I just need to search for them harder.

§

Ka was three years old when she learned to count.

– One raspberry, two, three…

She threaded raspberries on her little fingers, and then, opening a big mouth, gobbled them one by one, four, five… But just before reaching ten, she said *nine* and ate the last two at once.

I pretended to be cross with her:

– No cheating, sweetheart. Now, tell me, what comes after nine?

– Nothing.

– Nothing? No, my little monkey. After nine comes ten. And you know what, there is no last number, the numbers never end. This is called *infinity*.

Ka seemed a bit confused. She always looks so cute when trying to figure things out. She looked me in the eyes and said:

– So, then nine is infinity.

§

I died every night and was born again in the morning; I was imagining that I was a cat and had nine lives.

Nine is infinity.

our flat had one bedroom, a living room and a kitchen too narrow to fit in a dining table, so instead we ate on a small extending table in the corner of the living room; to save space, we neatly put away the folding chairs after each meal; for a long time the bedroom was the place where the whole family slept; my sister and I on the bunk bed, and our parents on the sofa bed they'd pull out each night and push back in the morning; the room was so small that, to reach the door, my sister and I had to crawl over the bed, careful not to step over our parents' feet

a week before my seventh birthday, our parents started sleeping in the living room, taking the sofa bed with them; I remember feeling as though a stream of fresh air had entered the room we could now call ours; the best birthday present I could ask for

the new sofa bed took up a whole wall and half of the living room, which was already cramped; a suffocating feeling was inevitable, so my father invested in two big mirrors, which he hung on the two opposite walls to make the room look bigger; he had that artistic flair, anything to do with music, art, literature; often people outside the family would see his fiery behaviour as nothing but artistic madness; he dressed up his loud laughter as being funny and outgoing, his shouting when arguing with others as being too passionate about the topic, his ugly words towards my mother as his own way of joking with no bad intentions

the first time I walked into the living room with the new mirrors on the walls, I gasped and froze, feeling intimidated by my own reflections; because of their position, each reflection would copy and multiply the image further, infinite times; my father's image was standing next to mine, as if following me in parallel dimensions, each one repeating itself

– isn't it great, huh?
he seemed pleased with the result, waiting for my acknowledgement
– it's nice
I lied, and rushed to my room while trying to collect and reassemble all those versions of me

Over the past few days I've been reading reviews of smoothie makers. I need a new one. I'm going through online reviews and star ratings, I ask buyers on Amazon for possible downsides and faults, I scroll down pages of other people's experiences and recommendations as if I'm buying something for life. I rarely make impulsive purchases these days. I like to plan ahead, calculate, collect opinions.

I think how much time I spend on choosing everyday items, and how often I make choices with little or no information when it comes to the most important part of my life: people. Ka didn't choose me as her mother, and I didn't choose her. Neither of us had any idea what it would be like to be a mother and daughter. We silently made a pact to be a family, to care for and love each other.

Babies are a blank canvas, and their immediate family as well as the community and the whole of society shape the way they are, the people they later become. But they also have their own personalities. Ka's stubbornness was evident from the day she was born; her quiet yet determined attempts at grabbing my attention when I got absorbed in another activity or thought were always successful. I like her the way she is, I love every bit of her, and yet I didn't choose her. I didn't read reviews about her, didn't collect opinions.

This is the case with relationships too, more or less. How could one know what's going to follow in the years to come, the way partners will change, the way you will change?

I cease these thoughts and go back to reading some more reviews.

§

– How are you feeling today?

– Loveless.

§

One Sunday I decided to make pancakes. My mum used to make them for me every weekend when I was little, almost religiously. Our little ritual to bring a dose of joyfulness to the lazy morning, wrapped in the smell of pancakes and blueberry jam. Or perhaps it was the only thing I ate with an appetite, which also made my mum happy. Now, being a mother myself, I felt the need to take over, to turn it into a weekend ritual for Ka.

I took an egg, cracked it with a fork and beat it for a minute. Then I added a pint of organic milk and a cup of plain wholegrain flour and folded them into the mixture. I reached for the hand mixer on the upper shelf, hardly ever used after a baking disaster or two, and whisked it all together. I watched the ingredients amalgamating into a smooth batter. The egg was not an egg any more, the milk was not milk and the flour not flour. They were all present and yet completely unified in their togetherness, transformed into something new that could only exist in the right combination of ingredients.

While pouring the mixture into the pan, I thought about me and Milo. Just like the pancake ingredients, our separate person-alities had started to lose shape in our relationship, transforming the *me* and *him* into *us*.

Just before I put the last pancake on top of the pile, Milo walked into the room.

– Morning, baby, I got up early to make pancakes. Ta–da!

– I wish you had stayed in bed a little longer and made love to me.

I placed the pancakes on the table next to a jar of blueberry jam and made myself a cup of strong coffee. Suddenly, I lost my appetite.

§

I long for love but my whole existence is engulfed by fear. The universal truth: you have to let one thing go in order to make space for something new. I know that, but the fear of it is too overwhelming. The idea of love, self-love in the first instance, wears thin and breaks.

§

Motherhood takes place behind closed doors, literally. Motherhood becomes the sum of the constant trepidation about someone else's life, understanding the baby's cry as if learning a foreign language, and responding to their immediate needs. Hungry, wet, tired.

Month after month, I started feeling stifled in the bubble at home, just the baby and me, days passing and blurring into weeks and months, divided by hourly tasks. Feed, change, lull to sleep. Going occasionally to the park nearby, I would find a quiet path so that Ka could sleep untouched by the noise. Then, sitting on a bench away from the crowded places, I'd stare at her calm face, her steady breathing, her fingers clenched in a fist. I would treasure those moments of stillness as the only time I could listen to my own thoughts as opposed to responding to someone else's needs. My brain was brimming with desperation and doubt in my own motherly abilities, constantly trying to sneak out through a secret door that I couldn't locate.

Hearing her sucking sounds in her sleep was a signal for me to dash back home to avoid the screams of hunger before the judging passengers' eyes. We would get home just in time to pick up our routine where we'd left it. Feed, change, lull to sleep. Before I knew it, Milo would be back, it would be dinner time and I'd slip into the kitchen to prepare a quick meal for the two of us. I remember feeling as though I was in a labyrinth I could not find my way out of, losing track of the entirety of the situation I was in, of the irreversible state of loneliness and isolation.

§

– When did you leave Milo?

– It was when, looking at him in bed sleeping, I realized he was not the man I wanted to wake up next to.

– But what made you realize that? Was there a particular reason? A quarrel maybe?

– Thousands of reasons, which I would hide from myself because I didn't want to see.

– See what?

– My father. In him. His desire to overpower me. To manipulate. The smell of arrogance, waiting for the right moment to burst out.

§

Over time I replaced the theatre criticism with book reviews for online journals and lifestyle magazines, the latter paying a bit more, enough for a pack of nappies. The money didn't matter; I was on a quest to save my sanity. But then guilt started to creep in. Writing vs nurturing, self-care vs caring for my child, satisfying my hunger for intellectual work vs feeding the baby made me realize that guilt is also a balancing act. Motherhood, with its child-centric routine, and pre-parenthood life when I could dedicate my time to personal interests and aspirations, were pushing up against each other, opening a chasm.

Life split starkly into before and after the baby's arrival. You're never the same after producing a new life that doesn't belong to you, and yet you're responsible for it. The mathematics of motherhood: you gain a child and lose a part of your freedom. For some, the expressions in the equation remain equal; they are in balance. For others, losing your sleep, your social life (initially, at least), your sanity, weighs more. Your career doesn't fully recover despite your ambition. You never pick things up where you left them before going on maternity leave. You keep reminding yourself that you love your child and that's the most important thing. It is, isn't it?

§

– Absolutely no way. You're not going back to work.

Milo's demand came as a shock when I told him about my plans.

He had his arguments. The baby was still too young and needed her mother; the research about how damaging an early separation is for the child; how going back to work would only bring more stress and exhaustion for me. I listened quietly; his arguments were strong. I was repelled by the singularity of motherhood. You can't be a mother and not be a mother at the same time. You also can't be a mother and something else: a professional, a creative person, someone who indulges themselves in late nights with friends and a rich social network.

I remember my mother working every day; I did miss her but never imagined a different option, didn't even dare ask her to stay at home with me. In my home country, all women work.

– Here you've got a choice, Milo said, as if reading my thoughts, a firm look on his face. Here, you don't have to sacrifice your child to work. I am able to take care of you, to provide for both of you, the money is good, you can stay at home with Ka and relax, baby.

That's what he said. To stay at home and relax. While he was working hard, partying hard with actors and actresses, producers, journalists, I was supposed to be grateful and keep my mouth shut.

– How long for? I asked, but didn't want to hear his answer.

– What do you mean *how long for?* Until she starts school, of course. Unless we make another one in the meantime. She's not going to be an only child, after all.

§

I stood there, shocked and completely numb. How had I not seen all this before? How had I not seen my father in Milo, his desire to impose on me, to decide for me, and to do it with such confidence and arrogance that it would blind me? While I was happy that he wasn't an alcoholic, finding comfort in the reassurance that he would never physically hurt me, I failed to notice all the other ways he was abusing me: amputating my freedom, robbing me of my personal space, distorting my emotional state.

That night I didn't go to our bedroom. I stayed on the sofa in the living room but didn't sleep all night. I was seven again, huddled in my loneliness in the dark, sobbing, snorting up my helplessness.

§

When I lodged the idea of him in myself, I didn't know how much emptiness would remain after he was gone.

When I was accepting his body every night, I didn't know how much pain would remain after him. Wet, sticky pain over my thighs, into my womb, deep inside my thoughts.

§

The fear started to crawl back. The next day, he bought me flowers, made dinner, made love to me. I was numb to all this.

The past, the present and the future lost their contours and amalgamated into a confused narrative, too difficult to follow. No matter how far I ran, I ended up in the same place. I didn't want to hate the self that I was going to create if I stayed, and so a decision had to be made. In a way, it was already made back then, but it took some time to come to pass.

§

One night, when Ka had just turned three, instead of a bedtime story I told her this:

– When you wake up tomorrow morning, don't be scared when you see the big black bags leaning against the wall, brimming with clothes, books, some toys and other essentials. Pretend they are magic creatures who have swallowed our stuff and will keep it for us as we move it to another place. Imagine this new place with its bright rooms, newly decorated walls which still leave a faint smell of paint, a balcony with lots of flowerpots, a small table and two chairs for our Sunday morning breakfasts. Imagine sitting there, frowning a bit at the sun before we give ourselves to its warmth. Imagine us coming back there every evening, cooking dinner and eating together, then falling asleep and dreaming beautiful dreams. Imagine how, over the weekends, we'll play board games, draw and make all sorts of animals out of clay, go out and meet our friends, invite them over and have fun. Hold on to this place, Ka, this is going to be our place. Our safe space.

– And what about Daddy, Mama?

– Daddy will stay here. Or maybe he'll live somewhere else too.

– But why can't he come with us?

§

Touring with his new theatre production, Milo was away from the city for a couple of weeks. It was my chance to find and rent a flat, pack our bags and leave. I knew it would be harder financially, but I had some savings and so the decision was made. A friend came on a windy Saturday morning to help us move, and drove us to our new place.

We parked on the street outside a four-storey building and dragged our bags and cardboard boxes to the second floor. Unlocking the door and finding myself surrounded by the emptiness waiting to be filled with new memories, gave me chills, anxiety mingling with a sense of liberation and excitement. It was a small one-bedroom flat with a balcony overlooking a communal garden with a few benches and a couple of swings, a playground I'd later find was enjoyed both by kids during the day and teenagers in the dark evening hours. It smelled of newly painted walls mixed with cleaning spray, the owners too eager to rent it out immediately after a quick refresh. The yellow-coloured living room felt bright and vibrant, despite the shadows falling from the opposite block of flats and drifting slowly to the back of the room.

We unpacked, found new places for our old items, went for a walk in the neighbourhood and grabbed a few veg from the nearby shop. Ka didn't talk much that day, only asked about her new nursery and cried when I told her she'd find new friends. I held her in my arms, feeling like a mother failing her child again, but there was nothing to dissuade me from my decision. I was supposed to feel happy and relieved, and partly I did, but I also feared Milo's reaction and awaited it patiently.

The moment he returned and found the empty house, he started calling and texting me, questioning where we were at first, then pleading for us to return and apologizing for whatever he'd done, and finally threatening to find us and to take Ka away from me. I waited for the storm to pass before I agreed to meet up.

Eventually, we did meet, shouted at each other and then calmed down, talked about it, about my need to have some space away from him. Only temporarily, I said, and this was the magic word that he clung on to. Before he let me go, we drank vodka like teenagers, talked some more and fucked on the sofa as though it were the first time, or maybe knowing it was the last.

I was learning to adjust to my new place, to the evenings at home, tired from work and overly stressed from the growing number of bills to pay, staring in the emptiness after putting Ka to sleep, alone with my hollow body, my words reflected back at me by a glass of wine. We split the items accumulated over the years and our common friends divided in half too, each one of them taking their preferred side and sticking to it to avoid awkward situations. Everything in my life halved, but slowly I started to feel more whole than ever before.

§

Breaking up with coffee while I was pregnant gave me headaches and insomnia. Quitting smoking made me restless, irritable and tired. For weeks I struggled, I couldn't recognize myself, I was very close to lighting that cigarette. I self-isolated to avoid temptation. I substituted cacao for coffee, eating for smoking. It wasn't easy, but I didn't expect it to be. Somehow, I was prepared for the bumpy road ahead of me.

Leaving Milo was like giving up coffee and cigarettes times infinity. I tried hard not to look back, not to compare my newly broken life with my parents' marriage and the consequences it had had for me. I tried not to blame them for my blindness about men, about different ways they can abuse a woman.

§

A letter, never sent:
'I'm learning to live without you. But how can I forget you, Milo? You left fingerprints all over my body; the smell of your

240

skin is all over mine, I still taste your lips, hear your voice, sense your thoughts, your whole being is etched over me. All over my body, traces of you. How could I possibly forget you?"

§

– Mama, will I get to know my father one day?

– Will he come to see me sometimes?

– Will he be taking me for the weekend?

– Will he give me presents for my birthdays?

– Will he send me cards from the holidays he'll be spending with his new family?

– Will he call me, by mistake, by the name of his other child?

– Will he call you dirty names when you're not around?

– Will he be my father, the one I have and don't have at the same time?

All the questions I don't have answers to

§

Milo moved to Canada just a few months after I left him.

– A terribly difficult decision, he said when he dropped Ka at the end of the weekend, and I knew he was already breaking our daughter's heart. It would be just holidays from now on, and not all holidays. He wanted to be present in her life but his girlfriend, some French twenty-something, had secured a new acting job, a golden opportunity for her career, he added, and I listened and nodded.

He called the other day to arrange things. Ka will be joining them on a holiday to southeastern France for the Easter holidays. They'll come to collect her on their way to Bordeaux, where his girlfriend is from. It will be the first holiday together since Milo moved abroad. My heart sinks at the thought. He'll be taking my daughter – also his daughter, of course – away for two weeks.

– What are you going to say to her when she asks you questions?
– What questions?
– Why you left her and moved on with your new life.

§

I decide not to dye eggs for Easter. You need someone to share the celebration; there is no point otherwise. Ka is with her father and his girlfriend. I need to learn to accept this fact and live with it.

I leave the house and take the bus, the first one that arrives at the stop. Fifteen minutes later I find myself in the area where I used to rent the basement studio. I jump off the bus and walk down the street. The dusty road, the Victorian houses with pretty plants in the front gardens whose scent hits me, the Turkish shop down the road with all the fruit and vegetable stalls on the pavement in front; it all looks familiar and different at the same time. I wonder what has happened to Kyron and his daughter. I deliberate for a moment, then take the stairs to the front door and ring the bell.

Silence.

What was I thinking?

I hurry back to the bus stop and rush home, ashamed.

§

The father–daughter reunion was as painful for Ka as I had expected. I regretted having agreed to him taking her on holiday in the first place but had no choice, lawyers being involved. Her questions about her dad and their next holiday together swamp me daily now.

– But why did he abandon me, Mama? Why does he live so, so far away?

I can't explain. I'm empty of reasons.

I'm feeling on the verge of existence. I know something has to change in my life, but I dread the idea of life altogether. Secretly, I'm hoping a car will drive over me, or that I will accidentally cut my veins, but such things don't happen when you wait for them. Then I leave these thoughts behind and feel pregnant with shame. It's not the right time. The girl starts school in September; she will need her mama to help her with the homework and to prepare her packed lunch.

§

I am in Bologna for a couple of days on a work trip, some new business pitch that took place earlier, and now I have the whole evening for myself. At the airport, looking for a bin for my empty water bottle, I came across one with a note on it: 'I feel so empty.' Clever, I admit, but those words evoke a feeling of emptiness in me.

I call the friend who is looking after Ka while I'm away. Ka wants to speak to me; she tells me everything that happened to her at nursery and makes kissing sounds. I find it hard to be separated from her even for a day. But I need to distract myself; she's all right and I'll see her tomorrow.

I walk down the streets and soak up the relaxed ambience. Elderly couples sitting on benches, others walking their dogs, mothers pushing buggies or stopping to have a chat with one another, teenagers laughing in big groups, their voices catching up with me as I amble. Nobody seems to be in a rush, everything happens gradually, like in slow motion. It's late spring and the wind is warm; it brings the aroma of ice-cream cones and coffee. I pass by the university, follow the crowds, and the street leads me to a square. People, young and beautiful, possibly students, are sitting on the ground, drinking beer and talking. I grab a beer too and sit on a pavement, watching all this from a distance, dazzled by the spontaneity of the moment. Their laughter, the smiles on their faces, the naked arms touching each other; all of this mesmerizes me, makes me want to be young and shallow again. The sunset gives the building a glowing orange colour and everything seems photoshopped, almost fake.

A feeling is slowly rising; a desire to merge with the city, with its sounds, echoes and shadows, starts to evolve. I imagine Ka and me living here, being happy and fulfilled. I let myself be completely engulfed by these thoughts.

The idea of relocating to a new city in which I've only spent a day seems a little impulsive, I realize that. No matter how many times I've moved to new places and have started my life from scratch, acquiring items, friendships and disappointments, I'm still looking forward to what's next, still secretly exploring the opportunity to go through the whole journey again. Running away from the past? Maybe. Looking for a way to forget? Most definitely.

I do believe that staying in one place makes you stagnant; moving around and moving away helps you think more clearly. If you want to find something different, you need a *something* in the first place, so the comparison can happen.

So if it's not a particular place that makes me want to move forward, what is it then? A vague idea is starting to shape, but I lose it quickly. Perhaps the answer is not out there, in these new cities, new people, new directions, but in me.

§

– Mama, when is Daddy coming back home?
   – He isn't coming back, poppet.
   – Why?
   (Silence.)
   – Doesn't he love me any more?
   – He loves you very much. He just… lives very far away.

244

– But maybe one day he will come back.

– Maybe.

I lock myself in the bathroom and take a long, scorching shower, the water mixing with my tears, burning my face, my skin. I stay under the water for hours, trying to wash away the toxic thoughts.

§

Last night I had a dream about Milo and his girlfriend. In my dream, the three of us were lying on a bed, naked. She had big breasts and short dark hair. He was licking her nipples and I was watching. Then she left, naked as she was, and Milo made love to me. When he finished, I looked at him. He had Kyron's face.

§

– You never told me the end of Soraya's story, Mama. She was living with Ivan in the village, they had a baby girl, but she was unhappy that he wouldn't let her go back to her friends in the forest. What happened next?

– You remembered it very well, Ka, well done. Now listen…

– For the baby's first birthday, Soraya's parents came to visit and to bring gifts, bread and honey to the mother and child.

'Let me dance for my old mother and father, Ivane. Let me dance for them just once,' Soraya pleaded with her husband, her voice sweet, her eyes deep like wells and about to tear up.

He couldn't resist and unlocked the chest. Soraya's face lit up. She put on the long white shirt and the rainbow belt and started dancing. Her feet were barely touching the ground, her thin body was swaying like an orris flower, and in one brief moment, before Ivan could say a word, she grabbed the baby, twirled around and flew up the chimney and into the sky. Soraya was finally free again; free to choose the life she wanted.

245

– Ka, it's time to sleep now.

– Is this the end of the tale?

– Yes, poppet, this is the end of the tale.

– But I don't like it. What about Ivan?

– Ivan never saw them again. He knew he couldn't have Soraya for long, as she belonged to another world. He was sad without her, but a few years later he married another woman and they had three children. A girl and two boys. The girl he called Soraya.

– And what about Soraya and her daughter?

– Soraya… I don't know, Ka.

– You must know, Mama. And if you don't, just make it up. It's your story.

– Another time, baby. Night-night.

STOP ELEVEN
Accord Junction

Y ou know when you wake up in the morning and have a feeling that the day is somehow significant to you, but you're unable to recall why? You pluck events from your memory, try to remember important things that could have happened on that day years ago, birthdays of relatives and close friends (the ones you remember anyway), the day you first kissed that guy you were crazy about (then he kissed your best friend and you tried to forget, but that date stuck in your mind like a wet leaf on the back of your shoe). Still nothing is forthcoming, and you keep searching through your mind, through all the pages of faces and places, you get out of bed and make a cup of coffee, try to distract yourself from the obsessive feeling hanging over you like a dark cloud, casting its shadow over your day, over your otherwise ordinary morning. You try one more time to untangle your memories; what about deaths, you think for a second, like a glance into a treasure chest you keep locked and only open when alone, deep in the night when people are asleep and the house is quiet, so no one else can see. The death of someone close, someone you remember, but somehow the date of their passing has escaped your overcrowded memory. May the twenty-third... And there you go.

Now I see the date clearly as if imprinted in my mind, the numbers and letters become bigger. It is written next to another, like a tail, separated by a dash, a short line that is there to express a whole life, a short line with a beginning and end, trapped between two dates. That's it.

It's been ten years since my father died. What should I think? How should I feel?

§

It's not the past that holds you back, but your expectations of the future, I grasped at last. I have a feeling that all those pieces of my broken past have somehow come into place, finally started to make sense and to make me feel whole. It still hurts; the rough edges are too sharp to touch but, placed next to one another, the pieces are less of a threat and more something I can look at from a distance. I realize that all my departures won't be worth it if I never arrive. And this arrival is not a geographical place but a state of mind. Perhaps I am ready to let go, to start again, to pack my bags and travel once more. This time towards myself.

§

I call work and ask for a few days off. Then I book the next flight for later that day, not caring that I'm paying a small fortune, pack a few clothes in a bag for me and Ka, and make us toast with peanut butter and banana for breakfast.

– Are we not going to nursery today?
She sounds disappointed.
– No, baby. We're going somewhere else.

– But where?

– Back, my sweetheart. We're going back.

§

We follow the sun in the sky and arrive before it has sunk down into the sea. I inhale deeply and hold the air for a few moments in my chest. The noise somehow ebbs away and I almost hear the waves, their gentle whisper of stories and times before we were here. The days are longer back home; I recall this well. The taxi drives us to my old neighbourhood and parks on a street next to ours.

– Roadworks, he says, and turns his bearded face towards me. It rained and flooded the street. There's no way I can drive you to that building.

– Same old story, I reply and pay him, telling him to keep the change.

We knock on the door and I shush Ka, so she keeps quiet.

My mum opens the door with the questions on her lips, her face looking concerned.

– You? Why are you here at this hour? Is there anything wrong?

– No, Mum. We just wanted to surprise you.

– You did surprise me! Come in, you must be so tired. Give Granny a hug, you little monkey!

Then, looking at me, she whispers:

– You could have called at least, so I could prepare a special dinner, make a cake, you know.

– It's OK, Mum. We had a bite on the go. You'll cook for us tomorrow.

The next morning we get up early. I don't feel like eating but the pancakes on the table look so inviting, I can't say no. Ka seems happy and spoons the blueberry jam over the pancakes, then gobbles them up as if she hasn't eaten for days.

– Granny makes the best pancakes, hey? I wink at her but she doesn't reply, just attempts a smile, her mouth full.

I leave them together and go into the room I used to call mine. It looks so different now. Our beds are long gone and have been replaced by a sofa bed in orange fabric with a fancy tea table next to it. The old desk has given way to a new one, looking much lighter and more comfortable. Across the room where our wardrobe used to be, there is a shelving unit nicely arranged with books, pottted plants and items collected on trips.

I put on my green dress, the same colour as my eyes, then leave. The sun is high and the day seems beautiful, although it is too hot already. I buy a pack of tulumbi from the supermarket across the street before getting the bus for a few stops. I seem to have forgotten this place, I haven't been here for so many years. I feel ashamed while searching for my father's grave for hours; I don't know who to ask, so I keep looking, my eyes hurting, all the names carved on the stones blurring. I find it at last. I stay there quietly, staring at his picture, trying to reconstruct the meaning of that little dash between the dates of his birth and death, listening to my heartbeat that invokes his spirit along with a new feeling, a feeling of purgation. Then, I open the pack of tulumbi and eat them all.

§

Back at home, Ka welcomes me with ecstatic screaming, pulls my hand and runs around the flat in fast forward. Our bedroom is a mess, pencils and clothes spread across the floor. My gaze is met by a scruffy teddy bear I used to play with when I was little; my mother has been quick to get it out of the dusty storage box in the attic.

– What happened? I frown and throw a look at Mum.

– Granny made us a cake! Ka drags me to the fridge to see for myself. Isn't this the best cake ever? she says.

The three-layer cake with chocolate filling and fluffy caramel cream on top is lying on the lower shelf, taking me by surprise. Memories flood in, my mouth watering already. Just then I notice a big piece of it is missing.

– Did you eat cake before dinner, Ka? What did we agree?

– No sweet things before meals. Sorry, Mama.

– Don't be so harsh on her. It was just a tiny little piece to taste it, wasn't it, Ka? my mother intervenes, which annoys me.

The rules she once enforced on me seemed no longer to hold true when it comes to her granddaughter. Back in the day, each object had its own place which my mother made sure never to change. I was never allowed to eat sweets, so as not to spoil my appetite; I could not paint or draw at home, so as not to leave marks on the table; nor to help her with baking, so as not to spill flour on the floor. All I could do was watch and pretend to cook for my toys. And look at them now, beating egg whites together, licking the cream off their fingers, laughing.

Since Ka was born, my mother has spent two weeks with her each summer. This means they've only spent two months together in total. It seems so strange to me that a small snippet of time can conjure this powerful connection between them. In a way, they're still strangers to each other, and yet there's my mother's readiness to cave in, to spoil her, to allow any behaviour forbidden to me as a child, to swallow so easily the things that used to irritate her.

I pour myself a glass of rum in an attempt to suppress my own irritation.

– Have you been drinking lately? my mother asks me after dinner when Ka is in bed and we sit in front of the TV. A Turkish drama is unfolding; I don't follow the series, but Mum wants to watch.

– I'm not drinking. I had a small glass of rum, that's all.

– Straight rum. Not even with ice. All I'm saying is, be careful not to turn into your late father.

The suddenness of her words stabs me. Have I accumulated traits from my dad which I used to despise? Will Ka be ashamed of me, the way I was embarrassed by my father? The thought locks my throat and I remain silent.

A black fly steals my gaze, circling around the lamp. I follow its erratic movements, the tiny little wings carrying the body in the air, buzzing. It hurtles towards the window then back towards the light, too close to the scorching bulb, mesmerized by its warmth and dazzling shine, perhaps. A strong fizzing sound and in a brief moment the grilled body drops on the table in front of us, lifeless against the white tablecloth. I look but don't move, as if giving it a chance to revive and take off. But sometimes there are no second chances.

– What a stupid fly! I hear my mum mumbling while scooping up the dead fly and throwing it out of the window.

Then she sits a little closer to me on the sofa in an attempt to reduce the distance between us, as if time has opened an abyss. The restless look on her face suggests she's preparing herself to ask me a question, so I wait.

– So how have you been really, since splitting with Milo?

– I'm OK, Mum. It was hard at first, but I feel so much better now. So much lighter.

– And are you, ahem, seeing anyone?

– No, I'm not, but that's fine. I don't need another man right now.

– Don't be ridiculous. We all need another half to spend our life with.

– Well, Mum, I'm a whole person, no place for other halves.

– You say that now, but you'll get older. Loneliness will engulf you before the wrinkles over your body do. You'll wake up one morning and you'll wonder why you didn't let yourself love again, why you didn't give it another chance.

Her eyes are on me, caressing me with love and reproach at the same time. It strikes me that only a mother can merge these two feelings into one. Did she mean to say this to me or to herself? Through the window, which my mother likes to keep ajar, the rustling of stray cats enters the room; they chase one another on the garage roofs. Then she turns aside and shadows overtake her face, the light contouring her silhouette.

– Stop biting your nails! How old are you? she scolds me, and I know the conversation is over.

The Turkish drama has ended too, and she hops through the channels until she stops at the ten o'clock news, then takes some plain biscuits from the cupboard behind her. We both feel an urge to confide, but the words accumulate and don't spill out. Each of us is trying to untangle the reasons behind the other's choices, pulling the strings of our thoughts in opposite directions.

– Mum, do you still keep that blue woollen dress you used to have? Remember? The one with the embroidery?

– What blue dress? I never wear blue. Blue doesn't suit my skin tone.

Her reaction surprises me at first. But she's right. Blue never suited her. Blue so often found refuge on her skin and under her eyes that it had become a part of her and she'd stopped noticing it. The colour faded away so that she could continue to live.

§

The next-door neighbour, an elderly woman I vaguely recall, greets us:

– Look who's here! The Londoners! How have you been?

– I'm great, thank you. How are you? I reply while stepping down the stairs, trying hard to avoid listening to the endless complaints that inevitably follow the question.

My mother scolds me for replying with such arrogance, as being humble is a virtue to be cherished.

I'm baffled, unsure of rules I've unintentionally broken.

– How was my reply arrogant, Mum?

– You say *great* as though you're the British queen. Just because you live abroad doesn't mean you should be showing off without considering other people's misfortune in life. You've completely lost your manners.

Later, I ponder socially acceptable behaviour here and there, tracing an invisible border and attempting to find my place somewhere in-between. I still haven't blended into British society, but I'm also no longer accepted by the land I used to call home. The layers of cultural and social cues pile up on top of each other and this metamorphosis pushes me towards the margins of each of the worlds I exist in.

Over the course of the week, we clash on everyday topics over breakfast, we argue about the ways she's spoiling Ka (and shouldn't really) during lunch, and we fight through dinner about corruption and the lack of Roma minority integration. We search for words to lubricate the friction between us and we fall asleep angered with the weight of guilt on our chests, promising ourselves to try harder tomorrow.

§

The next morning I wake to the clanging of spoons and pots coming from the kitchen. A moment later, Ka enters the room and starts pulling my blanket away.

– Get up, Mama!

I bury my heard under the pillow in an attempt to steal a few more minutes of quiet, just like when I was sixteen and liked sleeping deep into the day. The morning breeze pushes against the curtains and the sunbeams lick my cheeks.

– It's late. Hurry up, please, or we'll miss the bus.

The urgency in my mother's voice reminds me of the time she used to wake me up for school.

– What bus? Where are we going?

The day is warm and the bus is packed with elderly people, their curious gaze on us. In my bag I carry the packed lunch my mum had prepared in the morning, and we hold an empty basket each. The bus spills out of the city, drives on dusty roads through the newly constructed neighbourhoods on the outskirts. We pass small villages where the passengers are dropped off one by one, and an hour and a half later we reach a stop in the middle of nowhere, finding ourselves surrounded by endless acres of vineyards. Mum walks a step before us, showing us the way. It's a piece of land she's inherited from Grandma. The old vine trees seem dry and bony; the grass is so tall, it tickles our legs as we walk through it. We step ahead in silence until we near a small wooden shed, once painted deep green, the colour now eroded and the timber like flaky skin.

Behind the shed are a few cherry trees, heavy with fruit.

– What are these? Ka exclaims, never having seen cherries on a tree before.

My mum reaches out and lowers a branch toward Ka's face, so that she can pick the fruit herself. Then she hangs a pair of cherries on her ears and tuck her hair behind them.

– Here. You've got the most unique yummy earrings!

Ka's little elfin face lights up and she shovels cherries into her mouth, their red juice staining her lips.

– Grandma, these cherries are so, so delicious. Nothing like the ones from the shop back in London!

– I'm glad you like them. Now, shall we start a competition? Whoever fills up their basket with cherries first, wins.

Ka jumps for joy and my mum places her carefully on the tree trunk where it splits into three thick branches. She holds her there, encircling her small body with one hand while secretly filling Ka's basket.

I watch them giggling, singing at the top of their lungs, the May sunshine sneaking through the leaves and embellishing their faces. I stay still, breathing in this new, fresh air, the smell of soil, a feeling of homeland, a return to my forgotten roots. The vines look dead and abandoned, but the memories of this place are still alive, they creep in and take me back. I am Ka's age and my grandma is helping me climb the tree, placing cherries on my ears while I gorge myself on the ones I pick myself. They're sweet and crunchy, the day is beautiful, and I don't think about my dad, or fear, or anger. Unshed tears blur my vision and I hurry to take my basket and join the joyful racket.

– I win! I win! Ka screams and Mum lifts her down. Grandma, what do I actually win? she asks.

– You actually win a full basket of cherries, sweetheart!

– Just that? She pouts in disappointment.

– And a big hug from Grandma! Grrrr, I'm going to catch you now!

They chase each other and giggle, the wind carrying their laughter.

It's lunchtime and we throw a blanket on the ground next to the shed and place on it the boxes of food: boiled eggs, cheese sandwiches with butter and homemade bread, savoury muffins, stuffed peppers with feta cheese, slices of tomato and cucumber.

– I love having a picnic, Ka says while devouring the food. I love them because you get to pick whatever you like, that's why they're called *pick-nics*.

– Look at this hungry little girl! It must be the air, Mum says, and winks at me while taking a bite from her sandwich.

After we finish eating, we take a walk through the vineyards and greet an old man we meet who offers Ka a handful of strawberries from his basket, we pick wild flowers in fragrant bouquets and sit on a bench next to a stone water fountain, the engraved note suggesting it was built over five hundred years ago. We enjoy the peace, interrupted only by the buzzing of bees and insects.

I don't close my eyes; I keep them wide open and absorb the view, like a photograph that captures the serenity of the moment, so that I can return to it again and again.

Click.

§

She was the girl who kissed me on the lips one summer night infused with the scent of lilac trees, while we were smoking in the back yard of the restaurant where we both worked. I was upset by an earlier fight with my then boyfriend, and she had beautiful supple skin, weary eyes and warm breath. The kiss remained the only one, never repeated, never spoken of. Leah. She held sway over me. A quiet girl for whom meaning was not carried by words but by their absence. She abhorred her name for its biblical story meaning. Unloved. The name given by her mother the day she was born and surrendered for adoption. But Leah was never adopted, was destined to grow up alone, in care homes, dreaming of a life with a mother.

It's Saturday and I decide to call her. She seems happy to hear from me. We agree to meet at the park near the playground, so that Ka can have fun at the swings while we're chatting. The primary schools here break up for the summer holidays at the end of May, and the playground is crowded with kids, their clamour filling the air. Leah arrives with a little girl.

She is quick to introduce her:

– Meet Dara. And you must be Ka, hello! Why don't you go and play together?

The girls, shy at first, walk quietly towards the slide, both secretly examining each other, Ka copying Dara's moves. Dara seems to notice it and starts pulling funny faces, or teasing Ka to follow her on the climbing frame. A few minutes later, they are already friends, chatting and laughing together.

– It's so easy for the kids, isn't it? I say and sit on a nearby bench, still observing the girls.

– What is?

– The ease with which they approach a stranger, the way they start a friendship, or how they can laugh with someone as if they've known each other for ages.

– Dara hasn't always been like this, you know.

– What do you mean?

– See, she's in a children's home. I've been trying to adopt her for a couple of years, but the best I could do was to arrange for her to spend the weekends with me, as well as the school holidays. Now she seems like any other child out there, but when I first met her, she wouldn't say a word. It took us a long time to build that bridge to each other, to get her to trust me. It's our first summer together, the longest she's ever been allowed to spend with me, but I'm already dreading the day when school starts again and she has to go back to the home.

– I had no idea, Leah. Why haven't you told me?

– It's hard to explain. I've been going round in circles. Same old bureaucracy. The rules aren't here to help abandoned children but to complicate the adoption process. And being gay and single doesn't help much. But you know I'm determined. Dara is my time machine, a way for me to return to my past and reimagine my childhood.

We both pause for a moment. I think of the time I met her at the restaurant. I was doing night shifts while at uni, for the extra cash, while for Leah the job was her chance to build a normal life.

– If you need anything, Leah, just let me know.

– Thank you. I'll find a way. Let's just enjoy the moment, shall we?

And then, towards the girls:

– Who wants some ice cream?

I've always seen us as partners in crime; that crime was the pain we both endured as children. Thinking about her, I often see my own life, my own nightmares and shame about not having the same happy family as everyone else, fearing the stigma of being different.

§

On a bench under the shade of an old elm tree where I used to gather with friends when I was a teenager, I sit and say my goodbyes. I close my eyes and let the city penetrate my skin, to slip in with each breath and nest inside me. The smell of caramelized popcorn teases my nostrils and I indulge myself with the sounds of people walking on the street, the clattering of heels, the laughter of children, the faint clacking of metal bracelets from the teenage girls passing by. The whispers of this place that I both love and loathe caress my eardrums and I succumb to the pleasure they bring.

I am here and there, in the crack of nothingness that has enveloped me. I strip away the sorrow, and remorse, and despair. I remain undressed, my brain bare and pristine against all the hubbub around me, thoughts reordering, finally finding their place, decluttering. I stay here until my naked mind makes the sky shy and it blushes in nuances of purple and orange.

At home the bags are packed, placed diligently by the door, waiting. Mum calls a taxi, her voice trembling. She slides a bag of sweets into Ka's pocket and I scold her for stuffing the girl's body with sugar, but it's too late, Ka won't give it back. Earlier she attempted to shovel a jar of my favourite stuffed vine leaves and a bag of dried persimmons into my suitcase but finding any extra space proved challenging, even for her. Some things never change, I think to myself, but the taxi is waiting and I hold her in a brief hug.

We travel by bus to Sofia and eat overpriced sandwiches for dinner at the airport before boarding the 10 p.m. flight. Ka draws a picture in my notebook of her grandma, herself and me, then nestles in my lap and falls asleep, her head sweaty and heavy. A noisy group of boys shout over one another, visibly drunk and probably returning from a poisonous stag do, and I fear they'll wake Ka, but she's very tired and her breathing slows down, steady and deep.

Most mothers find their children's sleep peaceful, beautiful, their chance to have a quiet, relaxing time. It used to terrify me. Gazing at Ka's little body and calm face, bathed in stillness, would evoke an image of her being dead. Would she look like this? Her lucid skin seemed a shade lighter than usual. I would rush to touch her face gently to ensure she was warm. Still warm. Always warm. A relief.

Sometimes I try to imagine what my life without her would have been. Without that little someone who takes up your time, your thoughts, your space. Which things would have taken up this time and space then? What is the parallel life I pushed away like rotten potatoes to make room for the new life with my child? I think about this while sipping my big glass of Merlot and fail to see those other things. Emptiness. At other times I see myself as a woman with a successful career, with lots of jolly friends, people who want to share my company, find me amiable, amusing and benevolent. With a man who loves me and tolerates my period mood swings, my morning breath, my Marie Condo-style obsession with decluttering.

What's stopping me? Is it really my daughter who's keeping me at arm's length from this version of my life manifesting itself?

I attempt to read the book I bought the other day, enjoying the borrowed time the flight offers, jumping between time zones, stealing a couple of extra hours. We land late at night, having travelled miles and ages, yet somehow I feel closer to myself.

At home, I carry Ka to her bed and leave the bags in the hallway to be unpacked in the morning. Unzipping the suitcase the next day, a creased piece of paper rolls out on to the floor. I pick it up and unfold it, frowning against the gleaming sun reflected in the half-open window. A faint chime of church bells enters the room along with a stream of fresh air and purifies the stuffy room. In my mother's handwriting, there's a note inside:

I know you're not really into baking but for your little girl, please at least give it a try.

Caramel Cream Cake

Cake base

5 large eggs
180 g caster sugar
230 g white self-raising flour
6 tbsp sunflower oil
6 tbsp water

– *Preheat oven to 180°C (160°C fan).*
– *Line a deep 18 cm cake tin with greaseproof paper.*

- Beat the egg whites with an electric mixer at medium-high speed for around 3 to 4 minutes until stiff peaks are formed (the egg whites should quadruple in volume).
- Add the egg yolks one at a time and continue beating until the last egg yolk is incorporated.
- Mix the sugar, flour, oil and water together in a separate bowl.
- Carefully spoon some beaten egg into the sugar, flour, oil and water mixture. Once the mixture is well combined, add in more beaten egg, and fold in the beaten egg (combine the mixture evenly by lifting the mixture from the bottom to the top, in a folding motion). Be gentle and do not knock all the air out.
- Spoon the cake mixture into the cake tin.
- Place the cake in the middle of the preheated oven to bake.
- After 35 minutes, turn off the heat and leave the cake in the oven for another 5 minutes.
- Test the cake by inserting a skewer into the centre. The skewer should come out clean (if not, put the cake back in the oven for 5 more minutes). Turn out onto a wire rack to cool.

Chocolate Cream Filling

2 tbsp milk
25 g cocoa powder
40 g dark chocolate
200 g unsalted butter, at room temperature
300 g icing sugar
(50–60 g chopped walnuts, to add on top of the chocolate cream when assembling the cake)

- Heat a pan of water until it starts to simmer gently.
- Put a large metal or glass bowl over the pan, ensuring that the bottom of the bowl doesn't touch the water.

- *Put the dark chocolate in the bowl and let the steam from the hot water melt it, stirring gently. Once all the chocolate is melted, let it cool slightly.*
- *Beat the unsalted butter and icing sugar with an electric whisk at high speed until the mixture looks pale and fluffy.*
- *Add the cocoa powder and milk to the whipped butter and sugar.*
- *Add the slightly cooled melted chocolate into the whipped mixture and continue beating at medium-high speed until it is uniform in colour.*

CARAMEL CREAM ICING

Whites of 3 large eggs
80 g salted butter, at room temperature
90 g unsalted butter, at room temperature
200 g caster sugar

- *Beat the egg whites with 40 g of the caster sugar in an electric mixer at high speed until stiff peaks are formed when you pull the mixer away from the mixture.*
- *In a small pan, heat the rest of the caster sugar on a low to medium heat, stirring the mixture gently until all the lumps of sugar are dissolved. The liquid should look amber in colour.*
- *While the caramel is still hot, add it very slowly to the whipped egg white in a small trickle, beating the mixture on medium-high speed as you do so*
- *The egg white and caramel mixture should now look glossy. Leave it to cool to room temperature.*
- *Cut the butter into small (roughly 2 cm) cubes.*
- *Once the egg white has cooled, add the cubes of butter to the whipped egg white and caramel mixture one at a time and beat at medium speed. The caramel cream should combine and turn silky and soft.*

Assembling the Cake
(all the cake components should be cooled now)

- Carefully slice the cake horizontally into three equal-sized discs.
- Spread a layer of chocolate cream filling across the top of the bottom disc.
- Sprinkle about half of the chopped walnuts over the chocolate cream and put the second disc on top of the walnut and chocolate cream layer.
- Repeat the previous step with the second disc.
- Place the final disc on top. Using a spatula or palette knife, spread the caramel cream icing over the top and sides of the cake, making sure to cover it.

I run my fingers over the paper, tracing the letters, her imperfect handwriting, her perfect motherly love, the memory of the sweet caramel taste making my mouth water, then I fold the recipe in four and place it in between the pages of *Slavic Fairy Tales*.

§

– How are you feeling today?

– Ready. I'm ready to forgive.

– Forgive who?

– Everyone. My father. My mother too, for her choices I was unable to understand before.

– What about you?

– What about me?

– Are you able to break free from your past, wash down the feeling of guilt, and allow yourself to be loved?

§

It's the weekend before the school summer holidays. The girl is playing with her best friend at their house next door, so I have a few hours for myself. I put on bright red lipstick and dark sunglasses, and leave. Almost as if sleepwalking, I take the bus, and fifteen minutes later I am standing in front of my old flat once more, brushing sweaty palms against my skirt. I ring the bell. I wait. Ring again. The door opens.

– Hi.

§

He has grown a beard and lost some weight. His daughter is at university now, she's eighteen and beautiful, he says while I step into the room. I look around and notice things. I see my pictures hanging on the wall. He catches my eyes and smiles nervously, tries to mumble something incoherent but can't find the words. Slowly, we ease into something resembling a conversation and soon we chat as if we have never been distant from each other. It feels homey and comfortable with him. He speaks of everyday things, so we don't disturb our memories. He bought the flat from the owner, a two-bed flat too big for one man.

It's late afternoon and the orange sun, like a giant jelly bean, leaves warm traces on our faces. Kyron nears me and pulls up my top, kisses the side of my neck, my shoulder; it tickles, and I giggle like a teenage girl. We stay close, our bodies shy at first, rediscovering their forms and shadows, finding shelter in one another. Then, he brings a pot of mango and passion fruit sorbet from the fridge, with two spoons. We dig in, the sorbet melting in our mouths and dripping down our chins. We pause for a kiss, his fingers settling between mine, a familiar touch, and the moment stretches back to the time we used to smoke on the stairs outside the house, engulfed in silence. As though catching my thoughts, he rolls a cigarette and offers me one.

– No thanks. I quit smoking.

– Come again.

§

Come again, he said, and then, stay with me this time, stay with me in my flat, it's too big for one man, let me be with you and Ka, be part of your life, because you've been part of mine all along.

I laughed, as though he was telling the funniest joke. Then I asked him for a cigarette, just one, one isn't like smoking again. And I left. I picked up Ka from my friend, cooked dinner, read her a bedtime story.

She's fast asleep now; the flat is quiet and I can engage my own thoughts. I pull the blanket over her body and pause for a few moments before closing the door, listening to her steady breathing.

My laptop and a few book galleys await my attention when I return to the table I've turned into a desk. I take one book and press my fingers tightly over its slick paperback skin. No traces left, nothing on its body to show my presence, no signs of remembering our close encounter.

I open a bottle of Pinot Noir and sit on the floor, drinking from the bottle, looking into nothingness. The TV screen is black, empty, and I see my face reflected in its shiny surface.

– Stay with me. I whisper his words to my reflection as though to witness their truth. Stay with me. The words roll around my mouth and I'm unsure if I should spit them out or swallow them safely.

The night is warm, his eyes were warm, my thoughts are searing. I hear his words echoing in my head; his words are exciting and frightening at the same time, a dream I never dared to dream. Stay with me.

I let myself imagine what it might feel like to be with him, to feel treasured, to have my own space in a relationship. I picture this relationship, in which I make my choices and yet the man looks up to me, finds inspiration in me, never stops being curious about me. A friend. Someone I can talk to for the rest of my life and never get bored. A friend who picks me up whenever I stumble. A man who is not afraid to look after my child, knowing he will never be her father yet will raise her with me and give her his love and care, be there for her, a friend of hers too.

How realistic is this? I think. How much of it is a dream, and how much a possibility? Then again, a dream turns into a possibility if you let it become one. I realize that unless I explore it, this dream will remain a dream, locked and kept under the piles of past experiences, uncertainty and confusion, and sometimes, only sometimes will it surface in my sleep, in the long hours of the winter nights, and haunt me.

I fall asleep on the floor and wake up a few hours later, my body cold and stiff. I drag myself to the sofa and snuggle under the softness of a blanket. I dream of a house made from colourful Lego bricks, with a glass porch and big windows. No people are passing by; the street feels strangely quiet, eerie. I walk towards the house, climb the front steps and press the bell. Just as the door opens, the house collapses with a loud bang as if destroyed by some disgruntled child, turns into ruins and the Lego bricks start falling over me, crushing my body. Pitch black. In the darkness a hand approaches mine. I grab it, hold on to it tightly. In the darkness, I hear a voice: *Stay with me.*

The children's rumpus outside wakes me in the morning. My body is tense, but somehow feels light and ready to face the day. You were right all along; our past is here for a reason. There is no magic wand to repair the scattered mind, but there are ways to accept my past and to live with it. Love doesn't hurt; rejection does. Fear does. Loneliness does.

In the mirror on the wall, my face looks skinny and the skin creased. I follow the deep lines with my fingers, as though tracing a road that will take me to a better place. The pillow fabric is imprinted on my cheek; my skin remembers.

My body remembers, too.

It remembers the fear zipped under the skin of my seven-year-old self, the abuse she witnessed and the feeling of rage it awoke, the uneven shape of the marks, deep blue mixed with purple, and the weight of Dad's fist. But it has also learned how to keep going, how to create life and to give love. And, maybe, one day, how to heal.

ACKNOWLEDGEMENTS

Thank you to the women in my family.

My precious daughters, who let me learn from them every day. For being patient and understanding when I've been writing in pockets of time rather than playing a game with them.

My loving mother, for shaping the person I have become. For her nurturing power and for all the sacrifices she's made to create a safe space for me and my sister despite the turmoil she's been through. My journey starts with and always comes back to you.

My sister, for being my sounding board and pick-me-up every time I need her.

My grandmother, who was my saviour and my force. The Libra in the family, I miss her wisdom and balance. Thank you for the encouragement to keep writing.

I am so grateful to my wonderful publisher and editor Susie Nicklin for her faith in the book, for her care and guidance, and for working tirelessly on it with such perfection to make it what it is. Thank you to Alex Spears and the whole team at The Indigo Press who've been involved in this journey.

I'd like to thank Katerina Stoykova and her publisher Nevena Dishlieva-Krysteva (ICU Publishing), who let me read Stoykova's brave book *Second Skin* before anyone else, and who showed me that one can write about the ripple effects of domestic abuse on children in a bold, defiant and lyrical way. Thank you for giving me strength and inspiration.

And, of course, thank you to my husband, the person right beside me, who is always the first one to read my writing. You're my anchor. I love you and thank you for everything.

Transforming a manuscript into the book you hold in your hands is a group project.

Nataliya would like to thank everyone who helped to publish *Arrival* for their dedication, care and professionalism.

THE INDIGO PRESS TEAM

Susie Nicklin
Alex Spears
Phoebe Barker
Honor Scott

JACKET DESIGN

Luke Bird
Andy Soameson

PUBLICITY

Jordan Taylor-Jones

FOREIGN RIGHTS

The Marsh Agency

EDITORIAL PRODUCTION

Tetragon
Sarah Terry
Alex Middleton

RECIPE TESTING

Liz Kwok